ALSO BY JOÃO GUIMARÃES ROSA

The Devil to Pay in the Backlands
(*Grande Sertão: Veredas*) (*1963*)

Sagarana (*1966*)

THESE ARE BORZOI BOOKS,
published in New York by Alfred A. Knopf

❀ *The Third Bank of the River*
and Other Stories

THE THIRD BANK

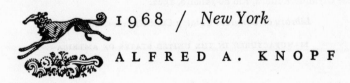

OF THE RIVER

AND OTHER STORIES

(*Primeiras Estórias*)

JOÃO GUIMARÃES ROSA

Translated from the Portuguese,

with an Introduction, by BARBARA SHELBY

1968 / *New York*

ALFRED A. KNOPF

THIS IS A BORZOI BOOK
PUBLISHED BY ALFRED A. KNOPF, INC.

FIRST AMERICAN EDITION

Copyright © 1968 by Alfred A. Knopf, Inc.

Library of Congress Catalog Card Number: 68–12682

MANUFACTURED IN THE UNITED STATES OF AMERICA

INTRODUCTION

THE FICTION of Brazil's great writer João Guimarães Rosa presents several obvious difficulties to the American or European reader. Compensated for many times over in surprise and delight, they remain formidable nevertheless. The language is exuberantly and elaborately experimental, the milieu is as Brazilian as the rosewood that gave the country its name, and the range of sympathy and variety of response required of the reader are enormous. The author is a sophisticated cosmopolitan who has lived in Rio de Janeiro for many years as chief of the Division of Frontiers for the Brazilian Foreign Office; but the setting of his stories is the state of Minas Gerais, where he practiced medicine in his youth. A linguist with as many languages at his command and as much linguistic freedom as Joyce, he re-creates the people and the backland of those medical days with the same stubborn exclusion of his longtime sojourns in Rio and Europe as Joyce's exclusion of Trieste and Paris from *Ulysses*. And to most

American readers, this milieu is thoroughly exotic and the richly elegant, flexible, and beautiful Portuguese unknown.

But as one reads—preferably aloud—the stories that make up what Rosa calls "first tales," the initial strangeness is replaced by a haunting kind of familiarity, and an American reader suddenly finds that he is at home after all—that the New Worlds, North and South, are more akin than he ever suspected and that what he hears in the work of this unique and utterly original writer are echoes and reminders of his own greatest writers. A measure of Rosa's stature is that the names that come to mind are those of our greatest and best.

Rosa shares Thoreau's and Emerson's confidence in the self-reliant individualist, the firm antimaterialist who keeps *things* out of the saddle. His hero, too, is the man who truly "exists," Emerson's "Man-Thinking," to whom nature and the intuition are the keys to knowledge. The tone, however, varies from the wild farcicality of "Much Ado" to the poetic seriousness of "Nothingness and the Human Condition." The sensuous delight that Thoreau takes in the thawing of the clay in a railroad cut near Walden, Rosa finds in the dazzling sun-drying manioc of "Substance," though no Concord transcendentalist could ever—more's the pity—have written the delicious love story in which Rosa lets the reader share his delight. The little hawk that Thoreau thrills to see in the April sky is not only beautiful, but also self-sufficiently alone and free and full of magic; the toucan of "Treetops," also, is wonderfully just these things. Thoreau plays games with mice and loons as partners; Rosa respects tiny green frogs and clever red cows, and enjoys them in Thoreau's own way.

What Rosa may substitute for huckleberrying expeditions is hard to imagine, but anyone who can tell the tale he does in "Hocus Psychocus" of the best play never written must surely be the same kind of magnet for little boys.

The only writer who loves the world and everything in it quite as Rosa does is probably Whitman. To Rosa, too, love means loving old as well as young, mad as well as sane, saint as well as sinner, body as well as spirit, place as well as person. He, too, can get inside the skin of a tree, or a young girl, or a spotted cow. He, too, sees "in a mouse miracles to stagger millions of infidels," and laughs to pray. He, too, is "in perfect health." He, too, "is untranslatable," "shaking his runaway locks at the sun" and "filtering and fibreing the blood."

There is also an obvious affinity with Poe, whose literary theory, like his practice, is still seminal and important in Latin America, as it is not—consciously, at least—in this country. Rosa attaches equally great importance to the sounds of words and is even fond of many of Poe's favorites—his immemorials and nevermores, those words with the long "or" sound which Poe thought the most melancholy and therefore the most beautiful. Rosa uses the short story in many of the same ways, playing as Poe did on the supernaturalism in common things and often approaching the tone of those prose poems and sketches full of haunting supernal beauty in which mood is more important than action. "The Mirror" and "The Third Bank of the River" use scientific, clinical intellectualizing to lead to the shiver, much as Poe did in his best tales of ratiocination and horror. But what one never finds any trace of in Rosa is the streak of neurotic cruelty and morbidity which colors everything Poe wrote.

Rosa's ladies with the great luminous eyes are lovable women or, perhaps, saints. They are never vampires.

Almost as often, and much more importantly, one is reminded of Hawthorne—the Hawthorne who wrote the story of the little Quaker which he calls "The Gentle Boy" and re-created the loving picture of his own little daughter in Pearl of *The Scarlet Letter;* and also the Hawthorne who wrote so often of the townsfolk whom he met at the pump in Salem or in his beloved White Mountains, the eccentrics, the "characters." Rosa has as strong a sense of his own home place, and often uses the same device of asking the reader to join him in exploring the mysteries of human psychology and of offering alternative possibilities of motivation, one of them mystical or supernatural, for the reader to accept or reject. Little Saint Nhinhinha of "The Girl from Beyond" and the hero of "A Young Man, Gleaming, White" are the most overtly otherworldly and the most preternaturally clairvoyant of his characters. They perform miracles; but even the most down-to-earth and practical actor in his stories expects and experiences them: Uncle Man'Antônio watches each declivity for a sight of the Mountain King; the prosaic elders who kill turkeyness itself to furnish a birthday feast watch for the miracle of the toucan's dawn arrival as faithfully as the boy. There is no romanticizing of youth as peculiarly wise, and every river has three banks.

But the writer whom Rosa is like in all his most essential aspects is Melville before the bitter failure of *Moby Dick.* There are the same vitality; the same gusto and playfulness and extravagance in the use of language; the same all-embracing affectionate sympathy for anything truly alive and itself, animal or child or man; and the same deep and transcendental seriousness. It is difficult to think of any other writer who has the same rare combination of characteristics. Some stories remind one of *Mardi* or such a story as "Las Encantadas"; more often we are back in the world of Queequeg and Pip and Stubb. Starbuck, or a Minas cousin, is here, too, as are cows and donkeys like small-scale Moby Dicks. If everything great in Melville—not only his characters and settings and plots, but even his metaphors—seems to have come out of those years from eighteen to twenty-five when the whaler was, as he said, his Harvard, Rosa finds just so many of the elements of his art in the backlands of his medical practice.

Though Rosa finds much that is antipathetic in Faulkner, to an American the great differences in their philosophies and the complete absence of abnormality as a theme in Rosa's work do not prevent Faulkner's constantly coming to mind. Aside from the same fierce love of one familiar place, they treat their child characters in much the same way: the little boy of "The Thin Edge of Happiness" and "Treetops" and the Ike of "The Bear" would understand each other very well, and Imp of "The Aldacious Navigator" would make a fine fourth on the Reivers' trip to Memphis. The tall-tale exaggeration of "The Spotted Horses," or any episode in which we meet Boon, is found in Rosa's "The Horse That Drank Beer" or "Notorious" or "My Friend the Fatalist." But the pitifully abused and dignified Marmalade Mule has her prototype, also, in the "Spotted Horses" incident. Both authors are preoccupied by the nature of time, and aspects of Rosa's verbal and syntactical manipulation remind one of Faulkner, though Rosa's tendency is toward ellipsis and Faulkner's toward accretion.

Translation of an author whose language is so primary a consideration is uncommonly difficult—even when the author himself is so obliging as to suggest such a title as "Hocus Psychocus." The inventiveness, the word play, the punning are formidable enough. But the alliterations and the rhythms and cadences set up by the skillfully varied repetitions of sounds and syllables can only be suggested except at the expense of sense. Erasmus learned Portuguese because he considered *The Lusiad* too important a work to miss; an American reader must learn Portuguese, too, if he is to experience fully Rosa's poetic power and wit.

Another great problem in rendering Rosa into another language arises from his ambiguities. Paulo Rónai, one of his most illuminating and sympathetic critics, perfectly characterizes Rosa when he speaks of "the humorous malice" with which "this courteous sphinx" refuses to explain, refuses to provide a key, "to give a map of the treasure." Successively, each of his books has become more densely, poetically suggestive, more involuted; and in a relatively uninflected language like English, many of the double possibilities that Rosa's control of his experimental Portuguese can somehow keep in suspension are —willy-nilly and with however much unwillingness on the part of the translator, who perfectly appreciates their central importance—resolved to some extent in the only alternative to the total incomprehensibility of non-language. It is like the problem every playwright or film director has had with "The Turn of the Screw." James could keep two possibilities in perfect balance; once seen on stage or screen instead of in the mind's eye of the reader, the pan falls inescapably on one side of the scales or the other.

Even critical comment may destroy some of the delicate ambiguities with which Rosa plays. To the Brazilian critic Vilem Flusser, "Criticism thins the density and transfers the story from the realm of life to that of the intellect." And in Rónai's words, in his fascinating introduction to the second edition of these stories published in Brazil, "Any attempt to explain it ends, however unwillingly, by filling in the outline of forms whose magic lies in the blurring of their contours, for it gives mathematical expression to a whole in which there are no perfect equations."

With all these problems of Englishing Rosa's work, whole continents of riches remain—of insight, of compassion, of laughter—especially for the American reader for whom the great nineteenth-century writers were a preparation for it. And this, not because Rosa is in the least old-fashioned or imitative, but because he, too, is, in his entirely original way, both great and American.

Barbara Shelby

CONTENTS

The Thin Edge of Happiness   3

Tantarum, My Boss   11

Substance   25

Much Ado   35

A Woman of Good Works   57

The Aldacious Navigator   73

Honeymoons   85

A Young Man, Gleaming, White   99

The Horse That Drank Beer   109

*Nothingness and the Human
Condition*   119

The Mirror   135

Cause and Effect   147

My Friend the Fatalist   155

No Man, No Woman   163

Hocus Psychocus   175

The Third Bank of the River   189

The Dagobé Brothers   197

The Girl from Beyond   205

Sorôco, His Mother, His Daughter   213

Notorious   219

Treetops   227

❁ *The Third Bank of the River and Other Stories*

THE THIN EDGE
OF HAPPINESS

I

THIS IS THE STORY: A little boy went with his aunt and
uncle to spend a few days in the place where the great
city was being built. The trip, which had been planned
for his pleasure, was, for him, sheer stuff of dreams. It
was still dark when they left, and unfamiliar odors hung
in the thin air. His mother and father came with him to
the airport. From then on his aunt and uncle would look
after him. Everyone talked and listened to the others,
smiling and exchanging greetings. The plane was a special four-seater belonging to the Company. Every single
one of his questions was answered; even the pilot talked
to him. The flight was to last a little over two hours. The
child, trembling with excitement, laughing happily to

himself, was comfortably cozy, like a leaf gently wafted by currents of air. Sometimes life seems to hover on the brink of some extraordinary truth. When they buckled his seat belt around him, the gesture was protective, like a caress, and then there was a new feeling of expectancy in the face of the not-known, the more-to-come. There was, the boy felt, a kind of growing, an expanding—as natural as the act of breathing. He felt himself taking flight into space. The boy.

Things happened smoothly, suddenly, all in accordance with a beneficent plan—one harmonious motion. Before he could feel a need, it was satisfied. He was given his choice of candy and chewing gum. With good-humored solicitousness, his uncle showed him that the seat could be tilted back—all you had to do was press the lever. He had the place by the window, looking out at the moving world. He was given magazines to look at, as many as he liked, and even a map, on which he was shown, now and again, where they were, what exact spot they were flying over. The boy laid the open magazines on his lap and peered out at the friendly piled-up clouds, the blue that was nothing but ether, that spacious brightness, and the flat ground like a map divided into fields and clearings, the green turning to yellows and reds and brown-and-green, and the mountains, low-lying, far off. Were they men, children, horses, oxen—those little bugs? The plane with its passengers flew supreme above them. The boy was living with absolute intensity; his joy threw out rays of light. He sat completely encased in the soft hum of the plane: that good, hardworking toy. Before he even noticed that he really would like something to eat, his aunt was offering him sandwiches. And Uncle was telling him

about all the games he would play and the things he
would see and do and the places he would go as soon as
they got there. The boy had everything in his mind's eye
at once, and nothing. The radiance and the long-long-
long cloud. They were landing.

II

The morning had hardly begun to stir. The construction
of the great city had just begun, on a tableland in the
semiwilderness: the magic monotony, the rarefied air. The
landing field was only a short way from the house, really
a wooden cabin on stilts at the very edge of the forest.
The boy looked around and breathed deeply, wishing with
all his heart that he could see even more vividly everything that presented itself in front of his eyes—so many
new things! The cabin was a small one; you were in the
kitchen before you knew it, and then in what was not
really a back yard but more like a clearing to keep the trees
from walking right into the house. The trees were tall,
and hung with lianas and little yellow orchids. Would
Indians rush out of the woods, or a wildcat, or a lion, or
wolves, or hunters? No, only sounds came. One turned
into a long trill of song, and then other birds began. His
heart opened to the birdsong. Did those little fellows like
to drink white rum?

Lord! When he saw the turkey in the middle of the
yard, between the house and the forest! The lordly turkey
imperiously turned its back on him to receive his admiring homage. It had snapped open its tail like a fan, and
now it puffed itself up and wheeled around; the brusque,

vigorous grating of its wings on the ground was like a
proclamation. It gobbled and shook its thick buttoned
armor plate of ruby-red wattles, and its head glinted with
flecks of rare light blue, the blue of the sky, tanager blue.
The creature was complete, sculptured, rounded, all
spheres and curved planes, with metallic green reflections
on blue-black—the quintessence of turkey. Beautiful,
beautiful! There was something hot, powerful, flowerlike
about it, a copiousness. Its gruff, thundering grandeur,
its gaudy self-importance, satisfied the eye and called
for the sounding of trumpets. Choleric and intoxicated
with its own splendor, the bird gurgled out another
gobble as it strutted. The boy laughed with all his heart.
But he had time for only one last look, for they were calling him to go for a ride.

III

They were riding in the jeep to where Ipê Farm was to be.
The boy repeated the name of each thing over to himself.
The ash-white dust. The savanna flower, the mastic trees.
The plushy white-sail flower. The green snake crossing the
road. The arnica, with its pale candelabra. The parrots,
like apparitions. The wild cherries dripping from their
branches. The white-tailed deer. The *canela-de-ema* in its
pomp of purple blooms. His uncle was talking: the place
was "filthy with partridges." There, a little ahead of them,
a troop of long-legged storks fled in Indian file. The pair
of herons. That wide landscape flooded by a lake of sunlight. The *buriti* palm at the edge of the creek where the
jeep stuck for a minute. Each thing took form out of

opaqueness to feed his ever-renewed joy, a kind of dreamy intoxication, and became a new and beloved possession, remaining perfect and pure in his memory like a castle ready-made and furnished. Each object was strange and unknown at first, only to be duly recognized in its proper turn. He was floating in air.

On the way back he thought about the turkey. Only a little, though, so as not to waste the warmth of the memory of that most important thing which was waiting for him in the clearing in the forest. He had held the ponderous grandeur for only one swift second. Was there one perhaps for each person, in each house?

They were very hungry; lunch was served and beer poured for his uncle, his aunt, and the engineers. Was it possible that that spirited scolding and gobbling could not be heard from the front room? This big city was going to be the grandest in the world. The turkey was opening its fan, haughty, exploding with puffed-up pride. . . . He could hardly eat his dessert, even though it was quince jam from their own trees, cut neatly and prettily, with its sugary, flower-fleshed perfume. He ran outside, eager to see it again.

Then, in a flash, it was not there to see. The forest was hideous and tall. Oh—where—? Only a few feathers, a few remains, there on the ground. "*Ué*, he's dead. Don't you know it's the 'doctor's' birthday tomorrow?" All eternity, all certainty, was lost; in a breath, in the glimmer of a sigh, that which is most precious is taken from us. How could they do it? And so suddenly? If he had known it was going to happen, he could at least have stared longer at the turkey. It had disappeared into space. In the infinitesimal null speck of a minute's time, a feather's

weight of death entered the child's soul. They were hunting for him: "Let's go see where the big city is going to
be, and the lake."

IV

He enclosed himself gravely in weariness and apathy so
that his thoughts would not wander. He would go with
them. He was ashamed to say anything about the turkey.
Maybe he shouldn't; maybe it wasn't right to feel such
poignant pain, such anguish and disappointment, because
of a turkey. But for them to have killed it seemed to him,
in some obscure way, a sin. He felt more and more tired;
unable to respond to what he was shown in the circum-
sadness: a horizon, men grading the landscape, the
gravel trucks, some vague trees, a stream with grayish
water, the white-sail just a faded plant, birdless, its enchantment broken, the air full of dust. His fatigue turned
from repressed emotion to secret fear: he was discovering
the possibility that there might be other misfortunes lurking in the mechanical world, in hostile space, and beginning to see that only a hair's breadth lies between contentment and disenchantment. He bowed his little head.

Here they were grading the landing field for the big
airport. Compressors, dump carts, steamrollers, a pile
driver ramming the earth with its pylon teeth. Tar trucks
crossed the wide, open field. How had they cleared away
the trees, his aunt wanted to know. They showed her
another machine, a tractor with a brush cutter in front, a
thick blade like a machete. Would she like to see how it
was done? A tree at the edge of the dense forest was

chosen, an ordinary tree no different from any other. The little man who drove the tractor had a cigarette butt in his mouth. The thing began to move, deliberately, in a straight line. The tree with its few high branches, fresh-looking, with light-colored bark . . . and then, suddenly, *rooh!* in an instant it fell to one side, all of it, every bit. It struck the ground so beautifully! The eye was not quick enough to capture the very moment—the silent shock—the full force of the blow. The boy felt sick. He looked at the sky—astonished and blue—and trembled. The tree had died with such finality. The clear slender trunk and the sudden, final tossing of its branches. Out of nowhere it lay there, guarding its secret.

V

When they got home he no longer wanted to go outside. The yard held a lost nostalgia, a vague remorse; he hardly knew what. The childish thoughts in his little head were still in the hieroglyphic stage. Nevertheless he went out after supper. And saw it—the unostentatious, sweetly unexpected surprise. The turkey was there! Oh, no, it wasn't. Not the same one. It was smaller, much less turkey. It had the coral color, the sumptuous train, the ruff, and the gurgling gobble, but its painful elegance lacked the hauteur, the rotundity, the taut, globular beauty of the other. Even so, its coming and its presence were some consolation.

Everything was softened by melancholy, even the day; that is, the coming of twilight. Nightfall is sorrowful every-where. The stillness stole out from where it was kept. The boy was soothed in a half-frightened way by his own despair; some inner force was working in him, putting down roots to strengthen his soul.

The turkey advanced to the edge of the forest. There it caught sight of—what was it? He could hardly make it out, it was getting so dark. Well, if it wasn't the other turkey's cut-off head, thrown on the trash heap! The boy felt pity and ecstasy.

But no. It was not comradely sympathy that had attracted the turkey to the spot. It was hatred. It pecked ferociously at the other head. The boy could not understand it. The forest, the black trees, were much too much; they were the world.

It was darkening.

Then a little green flight flew out of the forest, the first firefly. The firefly—there was a pretty thing! so tiny there in the air for only an instant, high, distant, retreating. It was—here now and gone again—happiness.

TANTARUM, MY BOSS

UH-OH!—THEY DON'T even give me time enough to hitch
my belt tighter and get my head under my hat, much less
finish the cup of coffee I was drinking quietly in the
kitchen. Then—"*Oh me . . .*" came the doleful voice of
the overseer's wife when the whole business began. I
saw what I was in for. Oh, sure. My smart Boss was making his getaway; he'd snuck out of bed and out of the
house quicker'n a bronco jumps over a fence, the sly old
coot. He sure didn't act his age, but the brains were thin-
ning out in his head, and his hours, or days, or weeks,
were numbered. Yep, and I've got to go where he goes,
got to be running after him all the time. So I lace myself
up, suck in my guts, turn myself inside out, go around
in tatters, jump over cliffs, tear all over the countryside;
that's what they pay me for. "Get a move on, Lightnin'

Bug, don't let the old man out of your sight!" the overseer
Sô Vincêncio kindly remarks, and I reckon he was laughing. "Just leave it to me!" I sing out, by damn, cussing him
all the time, and away I go, running hippity-hop down
the confounded wooden staircase in this rickety old ranch
house. . . .

And there he was in the corral—dancing around stiff-
legged as if he was on stilts, all worked up—fixing to
harness him a horse! I went right up close to him, following my orders; and he gave me a nasty look, worse than
usual. "I'm kind of needin' nothin'," he pushed me off,
making a face that would have weaned a baby. I nodded.
He shook his head, no. I nodded to the "no." Then he
grinned, half to himself. But he looked at me again, as if
he despised me, and remarked: "It's this way, my boy:
today's business is a mite too important for you to be
mixed up in!" That bothered me some and I really began
to wonder; his words seemed to weigh so much. I saw we
were off on the warpath, but with crooked swords, you
might say, and that he was off on a different kind of tack
from the usual. And we had just been talking the night
before about sending for the medical doctor from town
on his account, and no time to lose! And now the old
codger was telling me to saddle the horses. A fine piece
of jackassery! He wouldn't use our own gentle horses,
oh no! He wanted the burnt bay, a big tall horse you could
see was ornery, and the speckled black and white, who
had the same size and disposition. The confounded
beasts didn't belong on our ranch at all, but were maver-
icks we had picked up so's we could investigate who they
belonged to later. I did just what he said, as there wasn't
any help for it; to handle a lunatic it takes a lunatic and

a half. The blue of those big eyes of his went right
through me; he may have been crazy, but he knew how
to give orders. His beard was pointing up in the air—that
crisscross tangled beard of his without a single white hair
lying straight. He waved his arms around like a windmill.
He was better than a free sample.

I no sooner got my foot in the stirrup than he spurred
his horse and bolted out through the gate. With me—
giddyap, and the devil take the hindmost!—right after
him. There he was, tall and straight in the saddle, solid as
a two-by-four, proposing to do things and make things
happen. That's what it was to be a descendant of grand,
rich folks—*a Mr. João-de-Barros-Diniz-Robertes!* He had
been packed off there to the ranch in his dotty old age by
a passel of relatives who weren't about to put up with his
cantankerous ways and crazy doings in town. And yours
truly, being a poor man who needed the job, had to put
up with what was left of him. You can imagine what it's
like living with such a nutty old nuisance. It gets to me
and kind of scares me, too, besides shaming me before
folks. The burnt-bay horse was gaining, just burning up
the ground. He was a neighing horse, the kind that might
give you a tumble. Would the old man be able to handle
him? We were going along at a good smooth gait through
the brush, tandem. He had on a fancy ten-gallon som-
brero, and his long white hair—he still had plenty of it—
straggled out from under the brim. "Hey, let's go get
Skinny; I'll finish him off today!" he roared, out for blood.
Skinny was the doctor, his own great-nephew, who stuck
needles in him and washed out his innards. "I'll kill him!
I'll kill 'em all!" He spurred on, madder than ever. He
looked over at me and let out a yell that gave him away:

"When I cut loose, I'm the devil!" His red face shook; he was very light-complexioned, with those pale eyes I already told you about. He thought he'd made a sure-enough deal with the Devil!

Where'm I going?—now we were trotting, left, right, the horses stepping on gravel, their front feet slipping sideways. The old man had a good firm hand on the rein. I have to hand him that. But I wasn't what you might call easy in my mind. My job, my responsibility, is just to anchor him down and not let him kick up his heels too much. Waiting on an old beat-up guy, so decrepit I don't know how he manages to hold himself together! He was pretty far gone already; what if he fell down dead all of a sudden, then I'd be in a pickle, wouldn't I? It was always a case of having too little to do or too much; my old Boss fooled me every time. He scoffed: "Lightnin' Bug, so you think we're riding out today to make us some children?" There weren't any fishbones stuck in his throat and he didn't make any bones about what he said, either. Would he have the nerve to go where he'd see folks, looking like a scarecrow? No jacket, just a buttoned-up vest, dirty washed-out khaki pants, a low yellow boot on one foot and a high black one on the other, and his arm stuck through another vest that he said was his towel to wipe his face with. I hope to tell you! At least he didn't have a gun, just a honed-down, rusty old table knife; but he thought he could do in his nephew the medical doctor; he'd stick the dagger right through him—oh, he was fighting mad. But he said to me, slow and solemn: "L.B., my boy, go on back; I cannot have you going into terrible danger for my sake." Well, that was a good one. He thought he had made a deal with the Devil and was the biggest, bravest man alive, a bad man from the backlands. Well, he was a man all right—he came from real fighting stock—and he was my Boss! Then he began to point his finger, bang! bang! like a gun, but not making any noise. He pulled ahead, both of us going *rat-a-plan, rat-a-plan.*

When we got to a thick clump of trees we came on a dubious kind of fellow who didn't seem on the up and up, more like a man on the run. And he was mounted on a dubious kind of a horse. Whether we looked at him or not, he wasn't any concern of ours. But the old man saw something funny about him and rose up in his saddle, shouting through his plagued beard: "Evil will befall you!" He spurred the big horse up closer until he towered right over the fellow. It looked like he was going to manhandle him. And then, if the fellow didn't shrink back looking all rubbed out. Checkmate! I couldn't seem to get my eyes into focus, it was all so quick and queer. The old man jumping to the conclusion that the guy was a crook—and afterward, in Breberê, I found out he really was one, or halfway one, anyhow. That is, he was just a strong-arm, an outlaw's left-hand man, you might say. He didn't even try to make a move, but stayed right where he was; it was like watching a cat with a rattle. "Woe betide you!" went on the old man, shaking his big head; he wouldn't calm down. "Now pay for the bundle you've bought!" he preached. The outlaw's helper listened with all due respect, not knowing what it was he couldn't put off. Then the old man gave his orders: "You come with me, sir! I'll see that you get a just trial, provided you wear my colors and consent to serve me. . . ." And would you believe it? It's God's truth. The man brought his horse up close to ours and joined the procession. He hadn't exactly done it of his own free will, that's so; but he looked kind of hopeful.

I didn't even try to imagine what crazy thing would happen next; I was frying in the heat and fed up. It was clear the old man didn't have a scrap of sense left in him. He was damning and cussing and ranting and raving and lashing and slashing. And yelling: "Death to the poor and the unfortunate!" Did the old cuss think he was the Bad Man come to bedevil us all?

We banged along from pillar to post. The outlaw's helper wasn't laughing any, and I was even more leery. The next thing we saw was a poor unfortunate woman plodding along with a bundle of sticks, her baby on her back. My Boss edged his horse up to her, gentle-like. I was scared of what might happen. The old man swept off his hat, with plenty of bows and flourishes. I finally got my voice back: "Men, men, men! Remember the old saying: 'You can't hit a woman with a flower!'" That wasn't quite the way it went. The funny thing was that the old man's craziness seemed to be dying down. He treated the woman like she was somebody, and insisted so much she finally had to agree: my Boss got off his horse and helped her on, pulling the beast along by the reins as he walked in front, as gallant as you please. So our outlaw's helper had to pick up the bundle of firewood, and I had to hold the kid on my lap, the two of us on one horse like a couple of fools; can't you just see it?

The only lucky part of it was that the tomfoolery didn't last long, just to the next little town, where that poor, fussed-over woman was going. When she got down off the horse, she looked more embarrassed than grateful. But when you look twice, you see what a real good piece of foolishness sometimes leads to. The fact is that in that town there was a farm boy called Fuzzy, who was that woman's son; and he fell all over himself with gratitude when he saw his mother treated like a queen. But the old man, without giving him a chance to say no or maybe, commanded: "Equip yourself with a horse and place yourself under my orders, to go with the Devil and carry out a great act of vengeance!" I want to tell you something about that Fuzzy: some of his gray matter was there and some of it wasn't. And so what did he do but go off and find him a horse and catch up with us a good piece down the road. It was just to make us look like fools, all that monkey business. Us and everybody else who lived in those parts. But how could anybody act like anything but a fool with the old man's eyes glaring at us, one after the other. What ruination was ahead of us?

It might be anything. I'm telling the truth: I began to have doubts about my own good sense. Even time won't tell. But now we were passing through the little town of Fool'ya, where my cousin Curucutú lives. That isn't his real name; it's John Thomas Eyelash, just like my own handle isn't Lightnin' Bug, which is what my friends call me, but John Lightfoot Lucky. I spied my cousin and signaled to him. I just had time to say: "Saddle up your mare and make sure you catch up with us. I don't know where we're bound for, unless we're off on an errand for Old Nick." My cousin waved to show he'd got my meaning. And now we were right at the old man's heels—at a gallop. Off his rocker again. He flung himself forward in another spurt and yelled out: "I'll bring the world to an end!"

Mostly what we saw now was dust. High noon. Then

we veered off to Breberê; we were going to make our entrance in style. By fits and starts the wind blew the sound of bells in our direction. I remember it was some saint's day. Firecrackers were going off like popcorn, and you could see the bluish smoke in the air. The Boss stopped us all with a gesture, rising up proudly in the saddle: "This celebration is being held in my honor!" he said with emphasis; and the *ah-ching pum-pum* of the fireworks did sound like guns going off. None of us wanted to contradict him: the outlaw's helper; Fuzzy, the poor woman's son; my cousin Curucutú; and me; but I was only there because it was my job. We came into the town at a smart gallop, lined up behind him. Into Breberê.

It was the damnedest thing. The people were standing on top of each other in the huge church plaza, waiting for a procession. And the old man—he went right up to them, everything stopped, *pah!* and his big horse was prancing and kicking . . . and we followed him. Then the crowd went looky! looky! looky! and scattered and fell back. The old man dismounted and stood on his funny long legs; and we did the same. I had a half-thought as I wound the reins over my arm that we might be going to take up the blessed carrying poles of the litter that had the saint's image in it. But the old man fooled me again. He kept on going, shouting for the people to follow: "Good folk . . ." and began taking out what he had in his saddlebags. And he had plenty. He even scraped the bottom. It was money, lots and lots of the hard stuff, and he was throwing it on the ground. Oh me and oh my!—the ragtail mob squeezed close and got down on all fours "to glean some of that immortal dross." We used our elbows —we used our fists—trying to push our way out of the mob. Once we were in the clear, we got our breath back. But while all that commotion was going on, the priest came out of the door of the church wearing his vestments. The old man walked toward him. He walked, reached him, and bent his knee to receive a blessing; but before he got there, he knelt down a few times. "He has smoke in his head," I heard someone guess. The tall old gentleman with the soiled white beard was fanning himself with his broad-brimmed hat. "Did he get out of his bed so he could die in a holy place?" asked another man, who was Sky-Sniffer, the priest's neighbor and yes-man. He went on: "I won't abandon him, for I owe past favors to his estimable family." The old man heard him: "You, sir, approach!" The fellow nodded, saying to me in a low voice: "I'll hold onto a corner of the sail, and see him through to the end." A young fellow named Stinkweed wanted to come with us, too; was he out for the dough? The old man had gone loco again and was calling out: "To horse and to arms!" The priest smoothed him down with another blessing, holding out his hand to be kissed. I wasn't so sure of myself: "May God and earth be reconciled . . ." We mounted, took our leave, spurred and were off, leaving Breberê behind. The church bells rang out a tune.

All right—more galloping. No lunch under our belts, half the road still untraveled; that is, a road and a half. But with all that, *pah!* the old man was as proud as Lucifer. There on the edge of the king's highway was a gypsy camp. "To the left, ho!"—and turn off we did, into that tangle of dogs and children and copper kettles waiting to be mended. Those gypsies, with their sly, crafty, cunning ways; gypsies are never anything but barefaced. That's

what people say, anyway. These gypsies had a proposition
to make: they wanted us to swap all our horses. "Away
with you! The sign of diabolus upon you!" But when the
old man called his crew together, one of the gypsies decided to hitch up with us; a fellow called Nigger-Foot.
And what kind of tricks was he out for? I began to wonder
more and more when I saw so many people joining up
with us. Gouveia Full-Belly, for instance, who in worse
times had been a rotten soldier. Was I going to come out
ahead in this crazy game after all?

So on we rode, with the old man at the head of the
troop—ti-plocka . . . t'plocka . . . t'plocka . . . just like a
cavalry charge. Another addition, a hobo, kin to nobody,
was called Wood-Cutter, and spent his time loafing because he had an in. All eleven of us went with God: forward we marched—off and away, off and away—in bang-
up order. I saw my old Boss, like the king of the crackpots,
at the top of his tall tower. When we came to a stream he
laid down the law: "The horses can drink, but not us.
We must feel no thirst!" A devilish hard kind of temper-
ance, a penance for fierce men. My Boss, with his long
neck and big Adam's apple, a respectable figure of a man.
A warrior king! I may have been sick and tired of sweating; but there was something grand about the whole
thing.

"Death to the foul and shameless!" cried the old man.
The horses, the horsemen. At a galloping run. Thirteen of
us . . . fourteen. One more lad, the Fool, and one less, a
João Paulino. Then came a fellow called Kowtow, and a
friend of ours, anonymous by name; and, because he
loved fun and games, a colored fellow called Spotted Cap.
Each of them wanted a fling with the king, out of real

good feeling for that old man. We thundered on, scattered like straw in the wind. We were out for adventure; but more important than that, we just wanted to follow the old man. We were cocky and sure of ourselves; ready for sunshine or rain. We heard yelling ahead: "Death to the dead and buried!" vowed the old man.

He was what he was, a hero for all that, and would be when the curtain came down. "I'm on my way to the devil!" he roared. "I'll kill Skinny this very day, I'll kill and kill, kill, kill!" He hadn't forgotten his nephew the doctor in his rage. Giddyap! After all I'm not trash; I can understand seriosities as well as anybody. *Rat-a-tat, rat-a-tat,* we galloped on. We were well mounted! No one knew what we were after and nobody could make us stop. "Beware! Who goes there!" We'll go on a rampage! No, that's not the right word. At a gallop, the wind and the flowers. I rode up beside the old man— . . . *tapatrum, tapatrum . . . tantarum . . . tantarum*—and he said: not a thing. What moved was his eyes, a thicker kind of blue now, and they hit the mark. He eyed me a thousand times with one look. "Lightnin'!"—only that, but I understood from that one flash of his eyes. "John, Boss, it's John . . ." And there— *patrapum, tampatrum, tantarum*—I understood. Tantarum it was, then—that was the knight's name he'd taken: what do you think of that? Hurrah! We were riding into town in high style, on our high-stepping horses.

What's coming next?—I didn't wonder; and the old man kept shouting: "I'll kill him! I'll kill him!" Now the climax was on us. "To the doors and windows, all of you!" —tingle jingle jingle, all in a bunch. And I was right in the middle. Lightnin' Bug Lightfoot, Strong-Arm, Curucutú, Fuzzy, Sky-Sniffer, Stinkweed, Nigger-Foot, Full-

Belly, Wood-Cutter, Kowtow, the Fool, Spotted Cap; and
our no-named friend. The Old Man, bound to the Devil,
had all his flags flying. The very spirit of kick-up-your-
heels on Beelzebub's horns. And after-all's-said-and-done,
we were swept up the staircase, us daredevil clowns. We
were in the wings until the last act. Ah, here was the
street.

Catastrophe! The city gave us a funny kind of welcome.
Everybody in those streets, all crowded with cars and
soldiers, stared at our raggle-taggle troop with their
mouths hanging open. We weren't afraid a bit, we didn't
care about anything on earth. Oh, and our old racket-
maker, swearing death and destruction! Well, what the
devil! Let's go, boys. The Old Man knew how to find that
house, all right.

We were on our way and then we were there. What a
fine big house. And my dear, departed Boss in all his glory.
When I get to this part my eyes water. How did he do it,
how did he know? That very day and that very minute,
there was a party going on. The house was full of people,
all dressed up fancy-like for a christening: Skinny the
Doctor's baby girl. Without being afraid they'd make fun
of us or set the law on us, we swept in like a gust of wind.
Not a single soul—servants, guests, butlerman—barred
our way. They couldn't do enough for us. It was a party!

They were surprised, all right. The family gathering
looked pretty scared and solemn when they saw the Old
Man bust in like a corpse risen out of the grave, with all
the rest of us trailing him. The whole bunch was stocka-
block still. It was a little too much for them. They felt
guilty enough to be a little bit scared. And we were looking
at them pretty hard. The bow was strung mighty tight.

And the notch tightened some more. But then all of a sudden, the bow string snapped. In the silence the voice of the towering Old Man pealed out: "Dlong!" and raising his long arms, he said: "Give me the floor!"

And he took it. Would you believe your ears? It was a wonder. Do you know that everyone in that big, slack-jawed circle was willing to let him talk? Just think of that. Ah, and the Old Man, my Boss forever. First he coughed: Hrrumph!—and then he was off on a flood of words, so sincere you couldn't understand a single word, but his voice was so loud and grand, never stopping or dying away, like a rush and a rumble of stones. It was enough to make your head wobble on your shoulders. Made me want to bawl. My eyes were filling up again. And so were everybody else's, I reckon. The deeper they felt, the quieter they got. The Old Man had caught fire; he talked and talked. Afterward, people claimed that he'd just said a lot of foolishness, nothing but old-fashioned stuff. The Old Man seemed to get taller. Like a hero, with his dry beard and his old-timey way of talking. I knew his face, and I didn't know it.

He finally stopped, when he got good and ready. All his kinfolks hugged him. They were celebrating the Old Man's showing up in a big way. And all the rest of us who had been standing back were dusted off and handed drinks out of bottles opened just for us. Because the Old Man insisted that he wouldn't eat unless all his men were around him at the table, for we were his knights, his nonesuch troop, and had to wield knife and fork with him. Just think of that. We helped ourselves to the grub. And we drank, you know. The Old Man tasted a little of everything too, drank, swallowed, chewed with his very own teeth. He gave us a good smile, as he got ready for a long trip. He was happy. There was no Devil. No dead men.

After that he seemed to be waiting, alone in himself, apart from us. Sort of shriveled up, so little and so light: quiet as an empty glass. The overseer, Sô Vincêncio, would never see him again, rattling his brains in the dark corners of the ranch. Mr. João-de-Barros-Diniz-Robertes, that smart Boss of mine with his sad, knightly title. Now he was here he could go away for good; he had earned the right to a good rest. I choked off a shaky sob in the middle. Tantarum, then . . . Tantarum . . . That was a hero!

❖ Substance

Yes, cassava is the whitest thing in the fields: whiter than cotton, than an egret, than clothes on the line. From grater to wooden trough, from the kneading tray to the washbowls, a pulpy mass is gleaned and gleaned again, settling in the bottom of the water as a bluish milk—the starch—which is clean, clear, pure surprise. Her name was Maria Exita. Had he first seen her in May, or when? Maybe he thought of May because it was the month that had the best things in it: dew, the Virgin, clear light on the fields. Couples got married and there were parties: it was at one of them that he had noticed her, the flower. She did not at all resemble the gawky, thin child with her long history of misfortune who had come so long before to work on the Farm. Without warning the surprise had taken form. When a girl became so astonishingly beautiful, she must surely have done it little by little. But he, Sionésio, so seldom had any leisure time that he was never in the proper state of mind to be the first to notice such a transformation.

He had left the party soon after it had begun, having put in an appearance for form's sake. His life did not permit him to cut his sleeping hours short; he stretched when he went to bed so as to save time when he woke up. And then he was up doing—keeping his eye on each step by which the cassava root was processed into manioc flour and starch. The manioc products of Samburá were famous then, in that region and for miles beyond it. When he inherited the farm unexpectedly, Seo Nésio, who had been a lazy daydreamer until then, plunged energetically into the business as though laying about him with a whip, determined to outdo every other processor in the vicinity. He had planted vast acres of cassava tubers, which, incidentally, were the only crop that would thrive in that soil; he hired and paid laborers; in short, he made people open their eyes. He certainly could not have afforded to waste time on a little creature like her.

Maria Exita. Old Nhatiaga, one of the sifters, had led her in by the hand out of pity, fearful that neither her employer nor the other workers would make her welcome. For an evil fate had marked every door with black against the unfortunate girl: her frivolous mother had run off; one of her wicked brothers was in prison for crimes of murder; the other, equally unsavory, was an outlaw whose whereabouts no one knew; her father, a fairly decent sort of man, had been denounced as a leper and been hounded into a lazaretto, no doubt for the rest of his life. She may or may not have had some distant relatives: that is, she had once had a godmother who was wealthy enough to live in comfort, but she had only passed through the place once, and no one knew whether she was still living or, if she was, where. They took the girl in, nevertheless. Not so much out of direct pity for her as out of compassion for Nhatiaga. But they gave her a thankless job, the very worst one of all: she had to split the sheets of finely ground manioc meal on the stone slabs in the sun.

Returning in the afternoon, Sionésio rode across the planted fields at a canter and then at a walk, but always eagerly, looking in almost every direction. He never rested, even on Sunday, except on occasion at certain dubious houses where his body was comforted and he found rest of a sort. But he never tarried long. His real pleasure was in seeing, at the end of the day, the open cassava fields waving their green hands. He loved what was his—what his keen eyes embraced. But now he was only fatigued; self-absorbed. His saddle was scratchy with hard wear and the saddle-horn stuffing was showing through here and there; so many things needing repairs, and he had no time for them. Or even to go visiting at Ox Hill to see his quasi-fiancée and be steeped in her placid repose that was like the earth, in which all things were measured by distances. He was arriving at the Farm; but it was then that he spurred his mount.

Total quiet at Samburá on Sunday, the drying ground and the mill deserted, without their humming core. He had asked Nhatiaga where her protegée was. "She's splitting powder on the slabs," the old woman said tersely. What, doing a job like that even on Sunday? At least they could give her something else to do! "She's the one who wants to; she says she likes it. And I guess she really does . . ." Nhatiaga murmured. Knowing that she some-how belonged to the Farm and toiled there filled Sionésio with contentment; he was the person who managed things. He had no complaints. It was true that the flour-making was a struggle, a crude process; but he would soon be able to improve it a good deal by installing ma-chines, and then he could put out twice as much.

He had taken his time about going to see her. Waited until high noon—with a sun that birds flew away from. She was seated before a stone table on a little low bench; at that hour, she waited for new, hard, heavy blocks of pressed powder to be brought. So glaring white! It was horrible. It was torment, torture; you had to squinch your eyes shut like an armadillo's against the implacable brightness of the punishing sun at midday. The air hung quivering the whole day; you tried desperately to temper that staring white brilliance by losing yourself in some small black smudge on the horizon; and everything densely, intensely the same. He felt sorry for her—poor little flower—and asked: "What job are you doing?" A silly question if ever there was one, but it did not vex her. Only scarcely, barely, her lips not quite opened in a slow smile. She remained unruffled. And then, it was amazing to see that with her it was different: she neither tightened her face nor narrowed her eyes, denying them to the light, but offered them widely open—those luminous eyes which shone with a light of their own. She seemed not to suffer from the melancholy, sinister powder and the wicked glare of the sun, but rather to draw security and ease from them. And her beauty! She was so fair, so lovely, so exactly right, with her high color and slender elegance—a little lady, a girl like a waterfall. He found himself treating her with more ceremony than he had intended. He remarked irrelevantly that the manioc powder from Samburá was his pride because it was so marvelously white; that was why it was worth more to the Factory than the brown, ugly products of other nearby farms. . . .

It was after that meeting that he had learned more about her. He still rode horseback—but his heart was not mistaken—the Sundays were not alike any more. In the afternoon the doves and canaries began to sing. Well—he was the master—but he would not abuse his rights. "I found your ways to my liking, little maid . . ." he repeated what he might say in a future phrase. Maria Exita. Now he was familiar with the character and being of this girl who was so different from the others. That she had come to the Farm after a bitter life without remedy, the world against her, accursed, half-suffocated with loneliness. And then, of her own accord, without any discussion or hesitation, she had settled into that job—the thorniest, least desirable task, in that heat like the mouth of an oven, which numbed the fingers and inflamed the eyes with its dazzle. Had she been blown there as into a haven? She had no fear of the cruel, grainy powder, murderous to the sight in its unrelieved whiteness. Rather she seemed to take comfort in it as though it were a balm, a sort of relief in her affliction, a generous, wider hope. All that time. And her beauty; where did it come from? Her own, firm person? Her eyes were huge, and all sweetness. Her smiles were like angels descending. It was past Sionésio's understanding. It was good to know that she was happy

in spite of her harsh fate. It all depended on a gesture.
That is, if he did not behave ineptly and roll himself up
like a snail; he was in love, more or less.

"What if other men wanted her, too; what if she already cared for someone?"—the wings of this black doubt
swooped down on him. There were so many roving eyes
and hands among those who labored at Samburá; so many
parties—the idea gnawed at him. It hurt him even to
imagine her chatting with those who worked nearby,
encouraging familiarity. However, what he heard ap-
peased him. Even though her grace and comeliness
seemed ripe for love, she was protected from all their good
or bad intentions by an invisible shield—safeguarded by
the grave defects of her blood. They were afraid she might
have inherited her father's leprosy or her mother's light-
headedness and inflammatory nature. They were afraid
that one of her murderous brothers might turn up unexpectedly to defend his sister's virtue. They were cautious.
And so she was safe. But you can't provide for yourself
by trusting to perpetual guarantees. Sionésio began to
turn up at all the parties, staying from the beginning to
the very last dance. Not that he danced himself; he didn't
care for romping and roistering. He stayed off to one side,
his gaze fixed, like a vulture watching its prey. He would
not have believed that all of her actions could be so
exactly right—her quiet steps; the way she held her slim
waist in her hands; a moist, prolonged little pout, like
opening flower petals, a never-mourning dove. The same
maid who would be in front of the stone slab the next
morning, splitting the sun in the fragments, blocks,
boulders of terrible fine powder. When she danced she
danced well; but she was seldom chosen. They feared the

uncertain disease lurking under her beauty. Ah, it was providential, that impeding qualm. This way she was in a fair way never to marry, and could not be vain and frivolous either. She would be obliged to remain pure. No, he need have no misgivings. Maria Exita would be separated cleanly and without flaws on the slab of life, and would belong to no one else. No man should touch her.

And yet, he wanted her for himself, forever and always. And she would love him too, as surely as the sun.

But meanwhile there were the encumbrances of his unpredictable hours—moments snatched from between old hopes and new disappointments. He would go there, not at peace with himself until he had seen her; but he had a mordant way of admiring her, more or less at a distance. Maria Exita worked with both hands, either sitting on her low seat or standing up. She ministered to the fine powder—the burning-hot, singular substance, limpid dryness, sandy material—the massiness of that matter. Sometimes it was still wet when it came, soft and friable, sticking to her beautiful arms and whitening them to above her elbows. Wet or dry, it shone like the sun's self, with a reflected radiance that was too painful for Sionésio's eyes to bear. He might as well have stared the very sun in the face.

Those many weeks were a torment to him; as often as not he was unable to sleep at all. He was pitted against himself, consumed with passion, living a full-fledged romantic love affair. Suddenly at dawn he would start up to watch for threatening showers and jump out of bed, awakening everyone with shouts of "Bring in the powder! Bring in the powder!" They ran about in confusion and alarm, collecting sacks, buckets, and basins to fill with

manioc powder that was drying on the slabs, where it was
the only thing that stood out in the darkness, a pale, glim-
mering lagoon surrounded by afflicted creatures startled
from their sleep. He could hardly make out her form in
the dusty commotion, but he was content with her living
nearness, her warm presence relieving the soreness of his
heart. He heard them talking about her: "Wouldn't surprise me any if her mother came to get her some fine
morning . . . or her rich godmother. . . ." He was taken
by surprise. Without her, what was the good of throwing
himself into his work and exerting himself to increase
production and buy more land? He had to see her once
in a while; yes, he had to be with her—the only Maria in
the world. He would take his rest with no other women;
there would be no more distant sweetheart. He would have
to face the ordeal and the possible disappointment, sum-
mon the courage to try to make her his, put a fence
around his dream. Should he talk to Nhatiaga first? he
wondered, immediately swatting the thought like a mosquito against his forehead. It was not that he was afraid
of a refusal. He was struggling with himself, trying in
vain to turn something over in his mind in order to see
it clearly. The days went by. Pretexts and excuses slipped
away. What was he afraid of, that he could not put a
name to? A thought occurred to him: was he sound in
body himself? Was he good enough to deserve her? He
scrutinized his own wrists and fingers, rubbed his face
with his hands. At another time his temper was aroused:
he was angry with the girl. He wished to heaven his love
were a falsehood, and ended. So that he could be delivered from illusion, want something different—he would
willingly pay dearly to have peace of mind again and

look after his strict, though unreasonable, obligations and nothing more. But the heat and burden of his days engendered the anguish of his nights. He found himself in tears, and true. Why was it, then, that he could not bring himself to say here-you-are or there-you-are? Why was his mind so shaky, so sore from mulling over the matter with such grave deliberation? Why was he acting like a moonstruck dog? But he could not come to a decision! But the decision came to him.

The time was a little past nothing—between noon and one o'clock—and she was expecting him. Fearlessly, he asked her: "Are you willing to set the course of your life?" putting his whole heart into the question. "Only if I can do it right away . . ." and with her reply came a peal of clear, warm laughter which surely held no purposeful malice or disdain. The laughter in her impish eyes must have another meaning.

But suddenly the words he had heard made him wince, with a deep-rooted suspicion and doubt. What if she were like her mother? he caught himself thinking. What if her beauty—the fruitiness of her skin, so fresh and flourishing—were given to her for a short time only, doomed to thicken and grow scaly with the crooked, purple scars of the disfiguring disease? The horror of it made him stagger. At that moment he could hardly bear to contemplate her precious, deceitful comeliness. Unconsciously he surrendered his eyes to the manioc powder that outdazzled the sun as it lay on the slab. Though only for an instant, he found there a power of greatness bestowed, a dilated repose that reduced to whiteness the tumult of ideas tormenting him.

The luminous surprise.

The gleam of white.

Yes: but it was more. It was love—true, deep and sudden; above all else. Sionésio looked more closely, without shutting his face; he applied his heart, opening wide his eyes. He smiled at what was behind him. Maria Exita. The lovely brightness gave her succor. She—she! He drew close to her. He held out his hands to the strange, solar dust; the act of crumbling it gave him pleasure; it was like a child's game. They should all see him thus occupied, so that no one would remain in any doubt. And his heart lifted. "Maria, do you want the two of us never to be separated? Will you go and come with me?" He spoke as he gazed at the powder, an endless thing. She answered him simply: "I'll go, yes I will." She broke into a smile, which he did not even see. They were side by side, gazing in front of them, not even noticing Nhatiaga's shadow waiting quietly in the wideness of the day.

Sionésio and Maria Exita—half-seeing the refulgence of the all-white. No-act, no-time, stillness in their imagination. Only one-and-the-other, in-themselves-together, living at the vanishing point and never stopping, in heartship; heartfelt, heartthought love. White dawn. They advanced where they stood, within the light, as if it were the Day of All Birds.

. Much ado

ONE MORNING when all the cats were nice and neat inside their fur, I was standing outside the gate (which was against the rules) waiting for the newsboy to come with the papers, although I was officially on duty. Along with two or three other more or less casual bystanders, I saw a certain gentleman walk by with a rapid, precise step. Very temporarily, we received the impression of a man unsullied and undefiled. And immediately myth was born again into the world, for portentous events unfolded, exploded, filling our urban day with hurly-burly, hustle-bustle, and hurry-skurry.

"Oh, senhor!" was the cry, unless maybe it was a war cry—"Ugh, Sioux!"—which it might just as well have been as far as I was concerned, since I was either absent-minded or concentrating at the time, mulling over my own

personal quid pro quos, which are the stuff of life, to my
mind. But: "Oooh . . ."—had that well-set-up gentleman
stabbed some inoffensive passerby? I had an inkling in
a twinkling. No. All that had happened, as I half-per-
ceived, was that a not very skillful pickpocket had clum-
sily allowed himself to be caught in the act of stealing
someone's wallet. In a trice, with the erstwhile gentleman
as the trigger, our banal interior vacuum was broken open
to receive the imprint of the series of episodes which
followed.

"But he looks respectable, and he's well dressed, too,"
said Dr. Bilôlo's chauffeur in surprise, crawling out of the
car where he had been dozing. "It was a fountain pen he
swiped off some guy's lapel," testified the newsboy, who
had not appeared until the crucial moment. Finding himself pursued, the man ran so fast he left a streak in the
air as he tore around the plaza with only the front part
of his feet hitting the ground. "Catch him!" Well, rearing
up almost in the middle of the plaza was one of those royal
palms, maybe the biggest one of all, a really majestic-
looking tree. Now the man in his decorous business suit,
instead of running into it and without even stopping to
get rid of his shoes, flung his arms around it and clam-
bered up it with incredible alacrity, an absolutely sensa-
tional climb. Is a palm tree a palm tree or a palm tree or
a palm tree?—a philosopher might inquire. Our man,
not enlightened to that degree, had already scaled it to
the thin, sharp tip. And he managed to stay there.

"Well, I'll be!" I shook myself and blinked twice, trying
to get hold of myself again. Our man had gone straight to
the top of the mast, as light as a woodpecker, without a
single false move, and was perched on the very tip-top,

in the empyrean vault, as sassy as a *sabiá*. His pursuers
had halted, no less surprised than I was, and had come to
a standstill here at ground level, before the infinite palm—
the great Trojan wall. The sky was a flawless sapphire.
On the ground you couldn't even count the people in the
crowd, because its circumference was constantly being
enlarged by people swarming maggotlike into the plaza.
I certainly never would have believed that a crowd could
be generated so spontaneously.

Our man was, shall we say, ostentatious at that unexpected height: simultaneously flower and fruit. Our man
wasn't ours any longer. "Well, I must say he's artistic
about it"—this pronouncement came not from the newsboy but from the Chaplain of our Institute, and was almost
gleeful. The other observers sent up insults like kites,
clamoring for the police and the devil, and some of them
even calling for guns. Beyond their reach, very much
master of the situation, he hallelujahed gaily in mellif-
luent imitation. It was a wonder he could be heard so
well in spite of the distance. Was he giving a speech
about fountain pens? He was a street vendor, then, and
could spill a good spiel about fountain pens and ballpoints.
He hadn't chosen his territory very well, though, I thought
to myself. If it had not seemed unkind, I might have been
insulted at the idea of anyone's coming to perform that
kind of juggling act or acrobatic stunt right in front of
our Institute. But I had to hand it to him, he certainly
had a daring imagination. And I was only human: I
went over to see the spieler.

I heard someone calling me in that small space of
time and saw it was only Adalgiso, sobersided as usual,
except that he was tugging at my arm. Pulling and being

pulled, I ran across the plaza toward the cynosure, the center of the whirlpool. Because we were both wearing our white coats, the crowd opened a crooked kind of lane for us. "How did he get away?" asked the people, who cannot be fooled all of the time. Finally I was made to understand—poor, unlucky me. "How are you going to get him down?" Adalgiso and I were on duty that fantastico-inauspicious day.

That being the case, Adalgiso whispered a short, quick explanation: the man was not our patient. Alone and of his own free will, he had turned up at the Institute only a few minutes before. "Nothing abnormal in his features or general appearance; even the form and content of his speech seem at first to denote a fairly firm mental foundation. . . ." It was a serious case, very serious. Pressed forward by the mob, we were standing in the eye of the cyclone. "He said that he was sane, but, seeing that the rest of humanity was mad and on the eve of becoming more so, he had decided to enter the asylum voluntarily: thus, when things went from infernal to worse, he would be in a safe place, with enough space, good treatment, and security, which the majority—those on the outside— would eventually lack. . . ." And so Adalgiso did not even accuse himself of venial carelessness when he had gone to fill out his form.

"Are you surprised?" I avoided the question. Actually, the man had only slightly exaggerated a very old hypothesis: that of our own Professor D'Artagnan, who used to say that forty per cent of his students—us—were typical latent cases, and a good proportion of the rest as well, except that the diagnosis would have taken a little longer. . . . But Adalgiso went on in my astonished ear: "Do you know who he is? He gave his name and occupation. Sandoval recognized him. He's the Secretary of Finance...." All this in a low, vapid voice.

Just then the crowd fell quiet as if on purpose; it gave our nerves a wrench. It was sad to look up, where the sky was so clearly a high, scornful blue. In any case the man was a little this side of it, in a kind of ivory tower among the green, hispid palm fronds, at the terminal point of his rocket-rapid ascent. He was fulfilled, sublimely absurd. I know I am subject to dizziness. Who wouldn't be, under and face to face with such a thing, such a down-and-uproar? It was enough to make the hair on a wig stand on end. But there was no denying this: it was a superhuman individual gesture, a hyperbolic commitment, a herculean act. "Sandoval is going to call the Director, the Police, Government House . . ." Adalgiso assured me.

Now a palm has no leafy foliage like a mango tree; nor, as it happens, does it offer the stability and comfort of a pepper tree. So how on earth or over it could he contrive to keep himself up there so long, statesman or not, sane or sick? He was not perilously balanced; on the contrary. Cozily settled on the apogee, the foxy scalawag, besides acting like a lunatic, was clearly in no hurry whatever. The only thing he was doing was casting a shadow. At that very moment he began to shout as if delirious, knowing exactly what he was up to and no end pleased with himself: "I have never thought of myself as a human being!"—looking down on us disdainfully. He paused, then repeated the phrase, adding: "If you know me, it's a lie!" Was he answering me? He laughed, I laughed, he laughed again, we both laughed. The crowd laughed.

Not Adalgiso. "How could I guess? I don't know anything about politics," he inconcluded. "Manic excitation,
state of dementia . . . Acute, delirious mania . . . shouldn't
the contrast have been enough for me to get the symptoms
right?" he argued with himself. But, psst! who was the
V. I. So-and-So who was making his important presence
known? The Director appeared, advancing in all his full-
ness. There were policemen pushing the crowd aside to
make an imperial pathway for him and to prevent any
trouble—cops, guards, detectives, a commissioner, and
the Chief of Police. With the Director came the innocent
young male nurses and stretcher bearers, along with Sandoval, the Chaplain, Dr. Aeneas, and Dr. Bilôlo. They
were bringing a strait jacket with them. They stared up
at our empalmed man. Then the Director said master-
fully: "This should offer no difficulty!"

In diametrical refutation came Professor D'Artagnan
from the opposing side: "Hebephrenic paranoid psychosis,
dementia praecox, I see it clearly!" The two men cordially
despised each other, not only in a theoretical-speculative-
philosophical way, but also when it came to trifles. They
were rivals, as a matter of fact, although one was bald and
the other was not. And so, logically enough, the Director
replied unscientifically, but striking an attitude of dog-
matic authority: "Do you know who that gentleman is?"
and named the title in a hushed voice which was nonethe-
less audible to some of the nearby more sagacious members of the crowd. Professor D'Artagnan amended his ver-
dict: ". . . the disturbance is transitory, however, and will
in no way affect his civil standing . . ." and began ex-
patiating on the question of auto-intoxication versus infec-
tion. Even a wise man can be mistaken in what he be-

lieves—and the rest of us think we're wiping spots off glasses that are already clean. And so every one of us is a prepalatine donkey, or rather, *apud* the vulgate: a jackass. And furthermore, there being both logic and illogic in the world, the stretcher bearers did not deposit the stretcher on the ground.

For our exalted man recried: "Man cannot live!"—a slogan of his; and every time he was about to speak, he achieved a multitudinal silence from the thousands of people there below. He did not even neglect the art of mime: he made gestures as if he were balancing with a parasol. Was he threatening something or someone with his catastrophic creative impulses? "Man cannot live!" came the empirical, anhermeneutic statement out of the sheer egoism of logic. But he said the words not at all in the voice of a preposterous wag or a hallucinated humbug, but in a candid, generous tone. He was making a revelation which would benefit us all and instruct us in the truth, us substantial, sub-aerial beings, from whose milieu he had snatched himself. It was a fact: life itself seemed to be saying it was impossible. It looked that way to me. And in that case, it was necessary that a tremendous miracle take place unceasingly in every corner of the universe, which is what really is occurring, in actual fact. I could not resist a vague intellectual empathy toward the man who was now an abstraction—who had triumphantly nullified himself; who had attained the apex of an axiom.

Seven expert, official pairs of eyes studied him from inferior space. "What is to be done?" The Director summoned us to a council in a precarious clearing widened by the obliging Police after a preamble of billyclubs and blasphemous appeals. To our confusion, however, our illustrious patient was proving difficult. He embodied the soul incarnate of all things: inaccessible. And therefore immedicable. We would have to induce him to come down, or find some suitable way of unhoisting him. He was not in a handy position to be picked off the tree and was not the kind to be lured down with coaxing and strawberries. "What shall we do?" we all said in unison, but it took us a while to hit on a solution. Then the Director declared, with the air of one who draws and lets fly: "The firemen are coming!" Period. The stretcher bearers laid the stretcher on the ground.

Boos were what was coming. Not directed at us, fortunately, but at the guardian of our public finances. He had been pinpointed. The identity of our hero had been broadcast swiftly through the jostling mass. From the midst of it, from one throat and then another, in buffoonish, scattered shouts, the ready rumor sped; and one voxpopular version, which was shouted formidably to the heavens, was: "Demagogue! Demagogue! . . ." and Echo answered: "*Magoog!* . . ." the beautiful and the good; good night; my stars. What a hue and cry it was, that ultravociferate hallooing drawn from the multitude—standing chockablock, pitiless, parboiled by the March-day heat. I have a feeling that some of the members of our group, including myself, were vociferating, too. Sandoval certainly was: it was the first time in his life he had even made a halfway start at rebelling. Professor D'Artagnan reproved us: "Hasn't a politician the right to his mental disturbances?" in pedantic vexation. It was certainly true that the Director vacillated wildly in his judgments as a psychiataster when someone with

status was involved. As we observed him, we saw that
our poor man was fighting a losing battle: he had not
succeeded in hoisting his fame up with him to the pin-
nacle. A demagogue . . .

But he did finally succeed—with one fell swoop.
Gently but abruptly he began to move about, to teeter-
totter; and for good cause, for he let fall . . . a shoe!
Exactly, half of a pair of shoes—no more—with a lofty
condescension. It was a real theatrical coup, designed not
so much to intimidate as to pull off a hugely effective
piece of burlesque. Of course, there were fluxes and re-
fluxes among the stirring crowd when the banal object
was cast down from its height and came spinning gravita-
tionally in the air. That man—"He's a genius!" exclaimed
Dr. Bilôlo. The people sensed it, too, and applauded him,
and then redoubled their applause: *"Viva, viva! . . ."*
they thrilled with enthusiasm and turned themselves inside out. "A genius!" They knew he was one; they praised
him, gave him their oceanic applause. By St. Simeon the
Stylite! And no doubt he was a genius, a dramatic *per-
sona,* and an opportunist as well, who had, as was soon
to be confirmed, extraordinarily acute perceptions and a
fine sense of timing. For after a short pause, down came
the other shoe. This one described no parabola; it plum-
meted down as straight as a line drawn on a blackboard.
The shoes were a yellowish color. Our man on the may-
pole—the high-flown author and target of the electrify-
ing acclamation appropriate to his feat.

But the clapping was drowned out by sirens. The fire
engine made its way with some difficulty through the
crowd and emerged with a tintinnabulation of noise and
fanfare. And there it was anchored, ruddy as a lobster

sunrise. The cleared space was widened to give the firemen enough space to maneuver; they added to the scene
a heady note of belligerence which garnered the leftover
surplus of applause. By that time their Commandant had
come to an understanding with the Police and then with
us, of course. They had a second, longer truck which
formed the base of the ladder: the walking apparatus
needed for this undertaking, loftily deployable, essential,
a lot of machine. Now they were going to act—and to a
martial tempo, to cornet and whistle. They began. In the
face of all this, what would our patient say—our exposed,
conspicuous cynic?

He remarked: "The nasty's turning thingy . . ."
Cleverly comprehending our plans and becoming even
more intractable, he adopted a defensive mimicry, as ingenious as he was alienated. Our solution seemed not to
suit him: "I'll be taken in by no wooden horses!"—evinc-
ing a vigorous Trojan humor, suspicious of Pallas Athena.
And: "Do you want to eat me while I'm still green?!"—
which, being a mere mimetic and symptomatic phrase
(protective coloration, so to speak), neither clashed with
nor reinforced his preceding words.

The ladder aside, the stout-hearted firemen were men
enough to take the royal palm by assault; or maybe even
a single one of them, as expert in the technique as any
Antillian or Kanaka. And after all, they had ropes, hooks,
spikes, blocks, and pitons. There ensued an even greater
expectancy than before; conversation was spasmodic.
Silence set its seal on the crowd.

Not on our hero, though, who protested: "Stop!" He
made a gesture of further protest. "You won't get me off,
you won't get me down alive!" and he was in earnest,

oracular; his speech was skillful. Since he demurred, we had to hesitate, too. "If you come, I'll go, I'll . . . I'll vomit myself from here," he declaimed. He took a long time to say it, sounding very free, almost euphoric, as he skylarked about among the luxuriant palm leaves, almost losing his balance over and over again, oscillating by a thread. He added in a croak: "A barking dog isn't dumb." And now, if the skin of his teeth wore a little too thin, he would change from a warning into a subject for pity and terror. He seemed to be clinging with his knees to some narrowest knife edge: his palm, his soul. Ah . . . and almost, almo-o-ost . . . a-a-almost, almost . . . It made the roots of my hair tingle. Nix. "He's from a circus," someone—maybe Dr. Aeneas or Sandoval—whispered to me. That man could do anything, but we were not sure. Maybe it was a fake? Could he do the rope trick, escape from himself and from the devil? In his sly, harebrained obstinacy, he hung over a little farther, utterly pertinacious. We felt death's soft touch alongside us, stroking its stylographic drum. A panic terror gripped us; I froze. Now the crowd was fiercely in favor of the man: "No! No!"—the mob-cry—*"No! No! No!"*—a thundering tumult. The plaza clamored out its demand. There would have to be a delay. Otherwise, a reflex suicide would be produced—and then the whole problem would collapse. The Director quoted Empedocles. The terrestrial chiefs were agreed on one point: the urgency of doing nothing. The first attempt at a rescue operation was interrupted. The man had stopped swinging on the horn of the dilemma. He depended on himself, he, himself, he. Or on the deus ex machina, which, indeed, immediately appeared.

Ten . . . nine . . . The Finance Secretary's Chief of
Staff came up with the Chief of Police. Someone handed
him a pair of binoculars and he applied them to his eyes,
scanning the royal palm in front of and above him and
letting his gaze rest on the titular head; only to deny
him, out of humane respect: "I am not quite sure I recognize him. . . ." Making the choice that seemed most
fitting, he opted for a pale-faced solicitude. The air took
on the air of an antechamber; everything became increas-
ingly grave. Had the family been informed? No, and it
was better not: families only cause trouble and vexation.
But some vertical steps must be taken, and those were
left to our mismanagement. The demented man must be
parleyed with, there was no other way. Talk to gain time:
that was it. But how could a dialogue mesh on two such
different levels?

Would a scaffold be needed? No sooner was the
thought voiced than a conical tube was produced—the
fireman's megaphone. The Director was going to bend
his reasoning power to the cause: to penetrate into the
labyrinth of a mind, and, applying sledge-hammer blows
of his intellect, bring the fellow thudding to the ground
with the weight of his doctority. Curt, repeated siren
blasts generated an equivocal silence. The Director,
master of the dancing bears, grasped the big black
trumpet and brought it to his mouth. He pointed it up
like a circus megaphone and boomed into it: "Your Excellency! . . ." he began, subtly and persuasively; badly.
"Excellency! . . ." with an inappropriate subservience.
His bald head shone with a gleam of metalloid or metal;
the Director was fat and short. The crowd jeered unrea-
sonably: "Aren't you ashamed, old man!" and "Leave off,

leave off!" In this way the opinions of laymen only hinder the strategy of experts.

Losing his tone of command, the Director, all ready to abdicate, spat and was rinsed in sweat as he took the instrument from his mouth. But he did not pass the megaphone to Professor D'Artagnan, of course. Nor to eager Sandoval, nor to Adalgiso's ready lips. Nor to Dr. Bilôlo, who wanted it, nor to Dr. Aeneas, who lacked his customary voice. To whom, then? To me, me, me, if you please; but only as a last resort. I trembled as I obeyed, gathering all my wits. The Director was already dictating to me:

"My friend, we are going to do you a favor; we cordially wish to help you. . . ." I brought forth through the conduit; the words produced an echo. "A favor? From low to high?" came the sonorous reply. Well, he was as sharp as a needle, wasn't he? We would have to question him. And, at a new command from the Director, my voice called out authoritatively: "Psst! Hey! Listen! Look!" "Am I going bankrupt?" came his high shout. He was letting me go on, but he was obviously bored. After all, I was speaking of duty and affection! "Love is sheer stupefaction," he replied. (Applause.) He did, at times, deign to let out a cavernous "Wah, wa-wah!" with his hand over his mouth. And he cried tauntingly: "Can patience keep on sitting on its monument?" "Eh? Who? Eh?" shouted the Director impatiently, seizing the loudspeaker from my hands. "You, I, and those who are neutral," retorted the man; his imagination showed no signs of flagging at that incongruous elevation. Our inefficacious cawing, crowing, and cockadoodle-dooing, all our lovely verbiage, was only stirring up his gray matter to a demonic peak.

We left off, for better or worse, from what was the equivalent of trying to stir up a porcupine with our fists. From a long way up came the porcupine's final, perfidious question: "Were those your last hypotheses?"

No. There still remained the unexpected, the triumph of ipso-facto. What was coming? Who? The very man! The real Secretary of Finance, alive and in his right mind—ipso. He seemed to be emerging slowly out of the earth. Oppressed. Opaque. He embraced each of us, and we fawned on him gratefully, like the Prodigal Son's father or Ulysses' dog. He tried to speak, but his voice was inharmonic; he mentioned motives; did he fear a double? He was lifted onto the fire truck, then stood upright and turned completely around as though on a stage, displaying himself to the audience. His public owed him something. "My fellow citizens!" on the tips of his toes. "I am here, as you behold, me. I am not that man! I suspect the exploitation, the calumny, the fraudulent tricks, of my enemies and adversaries. . . ." He was obliged to stop because of hoarseness, which may have been a good thing or a bad. The other man, now ex-pseudo, deposed, listened idly. From the perch he had won, he nodded yes, yes, yes, without stopping.

It was midday in marble. Curiously enough no one seemed to be hungry or thirsty, there were so many other things to think about. Suddenly: "I have seen the Chimera!" yelled the man impolitely, inopportunely; his ire had been aroused. But who and what was he? Now he was no one, a nullity, nobody, nothing, no-man, nil. He had left elementary morality as a relative concept below him; that was all too clear. He was annoyed. And yet he was still pretending, in a jocose way, to be a castle in the air. Or was he enacting an epidermic epic? He showed us what lay between his shirt and his skin.

For suddenly, without waiting for the Secretary to finish his peroration, he began to undress. The fact is, he brought himself to light, drop by drop. There floated down on us, one after the other, his jacket, shorts, trousers—unfurled banners. Finally his shirt wafted down —airy, ballooning, billowing, white. What an uproar there was then—it was bedlam sure enough. In the crowd were women, old maids, young girls, cries, fainting fits, skelter-helter and pell-mell. The disrespectful public had only to raise its eyes, and it did—to behold him *in puris naturalibus,* like a white, peeled cassava root in the green tuft and front of the palm tree, a genuine naked man. Knowing he could be seen, he felt of his corporeal limbs. "The syndrome," observed Adalgiso; we were thrown into confusion again. "Bleuler's exophrenic syndrome . . ." noted Adalgiso, pontifically. The man was simplifying himself into a scandal and an emblem, a sort of magnificent Franciscan, by contrast with everyone else. But he lolled benignly, his good humor restored, in a truly primitive state.

In the melting heat the authorities sweltered and lost their tempers at all the high jinks. Could nothing be done about this disorderly, subversive, reprehensible citizen? They would have to go back to the beginning, they decided, after a confabulation: the horns of the problem would have to be confronted. The wheels began to turn, the brief, bellicose command was thundered out again, with fanfare: let the firemen perform their daring feat!

Our little arena and atrium had widened, roped off by policemen; and journalists were already milling about, a handful of reporters, photographers, and cameramen.

But the man was alert and persisted in his lofty intentions, in the guise of great activity. I could tell he was counting on perpetrating another hoax. He grew cautious. He was counterattacking. He hurled himself upward to still more horrible heights as soon as the rescuing began: he would not be rescued against his will! Until—yes, until. Ascending from the mobile palm fronds to the supreme vertex, he was about to attain the sharp point of the trunk itself and was in great peril of plunging headlong. He would have to fall—the thing was as self-evident as a waterfall. "Now!" was our ejaculation; what we felt was the opposite of lethargy. We held our breath. In the midst of all those separate silences, were the brave firemen advancing? Slyly the man shook himself on the topmost tip, swinging like a comic misanthropoid in expert balance on his own extraordinary axis. He blurted out: "Is my nature incapable of the leap from anthropoid to hominoid?" He certainly excelled in *hubris*.

Just as certainly, we were enjoying ourselves too. As though he still found it necessary to evince optimism, the man displayed an unexpected verve. He seemed almost to strut like a dandy. The pause was more complicated now, and worse. His impending fall and death hovered toweringly over us. But even if he fell and died, no one would understand a thing about him. The firemen were halted in their tracks. They fell back. And the tall ladder drooped, disjointedly, and was put back in its box. The diligent authorities, defeated once more, began to distribute tasks. I realized what was missing. Just then a

loud, lively band struck up a military march. From the top
of the palm tree, one solitary creature gazed down at us.

"Possessed by the devil," said the Chaplain, smiling.

Possessed were the students, certainly, whose name
was legion and who rushed up excitedly from the south
side of the plaza where they had been concentrated. All
hell's devils broke loose and pushed their way through
the crowd in a torrent. They had got it into their heads
that the man was one of their own; right or wrong, they
vowed they would liberate him. It was no easy task to
contain the ardent band. They brought with them, besides
their invisible banner, a hereditary fervor. They were pig-
headed, too. Would squadrons of rampant horsemen come
into action against the noble young people? Would they
attack? Well, later. The confusion was greater than ever.
Everything tended to evolve with the dizzying speed of
revelation. Eventually reinforcements were requested,
with a view to clearing the plaza; and it was none too
soon. Unnational anthems were being chanted, spreading to the multi-mob. And where was peace?

From ace to joker to king, the Secretary of Law and
Justice watched the hubbub from atop the fire truck.
Stentorian and bulky, he wasted no time making jokes:
"Young men! I know you like to hear me. I'll promise anything. . . ." and it was true. They applauded him for it
rebukingly, trusting his past record. Then there was a
remission, and some measure of calm. In the confusion
of yeses and noes, the Finance Secretary, worn out with
a variety of emotions, escaped and made his way to pri-
vate life.

Nothing else happened. The man could be glimpsed as
he settled down among the palm leaves as though they

were a cradle. What if he went to sleep or loosened his grip, grew torpid, and finally fell and was smashed to smithereens? Professor D'Artagnan undertook to explain to his circumstanding audience how the fellow was able to remain firmly in place for such an unconscionable length of time. He was taking advantage of our patience —a hebephrenic catatonic—a stereotyped attitude. "Among the Paressí or Nhambiquara Indians, he would soon be felled by arrows," concluded Dr. Bilôlo, satisfied to find that civilization nurtures human solidarity. For even the Director and Professor D'Artagnan, both sincere and rational by this time, were being pleasant to each other.

Now a new invention was born of old necessity. Three times mad as the man was, would he not listen to the appeal of some nearby, discreet argument, and condescend? To make sure he would not become skittish, they consulted him and he agreed to listen. And the deed was plotted and grew wings: the exploratory ladder, like a kangaroo or a huge red praying mantis, expanded into a contraption that reached more than halfway to the top of the tree. It was ascended by our daring, dauntless Director, newly naturalized a hero. Up I went after him, like Dante descending behind Virgil. The firemen helped us up. We addressed the man in the gallery, disoriented in space ourselves. Many yards above us still, he listened to us waste our Latin. Why, then, did he suddenly shout brusquely for "Help!"?

There was more hubbub and commotion—and the lower world exploded. In fury, tumult, and frenzy, the crowd grew ever more unreasonable and irrational, responding to a thousand influences, a prey to delusions

and ready for the madhouse. I prayed as hard as I could
that they would not overturn fire engine and ladder. And
all because of the above-said so-and-so; it was as if he
had poisoned the city reservoirs.

The strange and human reappeared. The man, I see
that he is visible; I have to notice him. And suddenly a
terrible thing happened. He tried to speak, but his voice
broke and died away. His reason was in equilibrium
again: that is, he was lucid, naked, and hanging. Worse
than lucid: elucidated, with his head screwed on tight
again. He was awake! His access of madness, then, had
worn off by itself and he had awakened from delirium
to find that he had been walking in his sleep. He was
delivered from the promptings of influences and intui-
tions; had merely, with a sick consciousness, detumesced
his mind, retreating to what was real and autonomous,
to the bad stretch of space and time, to never-ending
moderation. The poor man's heart almost jumped out of
his breast. And he felt fear and horror, at finding himself
so newly human. He no doubt experienced a retrogressive
fright at what he had so lately been able to do, danger-
ously and at high cost, when he was out of step, his intelligence becalmed. And now he might precipitate himself, from one moment to none. I trembled in sympathy.
Would he fall over the edge? We shivered. It was an
impasse. The fact is, he was himself again; and he was
thinking. And suffering—from shame and acrophobia.
Infinitely far below him the base mob ululated, a mad,
infernal sea.

How was he to get out of his predicament, now that he
had turned the staid town inside out? I understood him.
He had neither the face nor the clothes—this buffoon,

runaway, wretch—with which to present himself for the final judgment. He hesitated, galvanized. Would he choose not to be saved, then? In the drama on the catafalque, the hero's cup was turned down. A man is, above all, irreversible. He saw himself dotting the misty sphere in some other, immeasurable distance, in the form of millions and trillions of palm trees. Did he find himself being propelled into space, poor man, and attempting to cling, in vain, to Absolute Reason? The raving mob—exalted, maddened—had sensed as much and turned against the man who had somehow deprived us of some marvelous sequel. And so they howled. Fiercely, ferociously. He was sane. The maniacs wanted to lynch him.

That man inspired a pity that was outside the human province. The necessity to live was defeating him. Now, like an opossum feigning death, he sought our aid. He was easy prey for the firemen, who hastened to make him reappear in an act of prestidigitation. They lowered him with the help of planks, ropes, and other apocatastatic means. At least he was safe. Just like that. For now. But would the crowd destroy him?

Denouement: Perched on the ladder as it was still descending, he looked more closely at the deogenesic, Diogenistic mob. As he gazed at it, something unexpected took place in his head. He offered us another color. Had the people maddened him again? He merely proclaimed: "Long live the struggle! Long live Freedom!"—a naked, adamic psychiatrist. He received a frantic ovation; tens of thousands were overcome with emotion. He waved and reached the ground unscathed. Picking up his soul from between his feet, he became another man. He stood erect, definitive, and nude.

The upshot was magnificent. They lifted him to their shoulders and bore him away in splendor. He smiled, and doubtless proffered a remark or two, or none. No one could have stopped anyone else in that commotion of the people for the people. Everything fell apart as it happened, sprawling into triviality. The day had been lived out. Only the royal palm remained, unchanged, unreal.

Conclusion: After it was all over, the glow extinguished, we exchanged our white coats for jackets. Drastic steps to be taken in the future were discussed, with variations, by the ex-professo Professor D'Artagnan and the Director and Dr. Aeneas, alienists. "I see that I still haven't really seen what I saw," observed Sandoval, full of historical skepticism. "Life is a continuous progression into the unknown," explained Dr. Bilôlo—serious, I think, for the first time. He donned his hat elegantly, since he could be sure of nothing. Life was of the moment.

Only Adalgiso said nothing. Now, for no apparent reason, he made us uneasy. Sober, correct, all too circumspect; and terribly, unsatisfactorily, not himself. In our shared dream, he had remained insoluble. I felt a reminiscent, animal chill. He did not say anything. Or maybe he did, in line with everything else, and that was all. And he went to town for a plate of shrimp.

❖ A WOMAN OF
GOOD WORKS

I know nobody here ever paid any attention to the woman; it was not likely that they should. People live so close together in a little place like this, like impotent shadows, that they take other people's habits for granted. And when someone doesn't seem interesting enough to bother about, they stop noticing him at all. But do you really believe that she wasn't worth troubling about? If you do—well, it's because you've never really thought about her at all, or wondered much about her, either. After all, why should you? The woman—dressed in rags, stinking, filthy, pitiful, as well as old and ugly, and half crazy because of a crime of which she'd never repented— was a blind man's guide. None of you ever suspected, did you, that she might have taken on a burden too heavy for anyone to bear?

One would think you might at least have known her
name; but when I asked, no one could say it properly.
They just called that despised woman Marmalade Mule.
The pains in her hips made her walk stooped over, her
knees sticking out in front. She seemed to carry her own
tangled forest around with her even when she was out
in the open, walking down the street. No spot she passed
ever looked as if it gave her enough room for comfort.
What was most pitiable about her was her flatness—she
was achingly thin, like a long lean skeleton, as if leeches
had sucked all her blood away; with those eyes that
wouldn't look at you, that hair like a wolf's pelt, that face;
shadows could bring out no hollows, no relief. Wasn't
what made you afraid of her her hungry jaws, her secret
witch's ways? But—sometimes her chin trembled. And
one should note also her tiptoeing, gingerly walk like that
of a solitary mare, and her sham savagery. Let's not dis-
regard any of the facts.

You didn't even suspect, eh? That you might have been
wrong about everything and in everything you believed?
You used to say, didn't you, that she hoarded coins she
plundered from what the blind man collected; but if she
had any such fortune in money, her fate was not only
not a fortunate one, it was most terrible. However ugly
and disreputable she was, you would have understood
how terrible if you had been able to find her real features
under all that sordid disarray of stain and coarseness, and
perceived that her wrinkles came from her drawn expression and not from age. Remember her as she really was;
try very hard to. Weigh her sparse words, her gestures, a
few of the things she did, and you'll find that she was
actually shrewd, made alert and keen-witted by her very

misfortunes. And her old crime—? Well, according to what I heard, the man she murdered was a villain, a cur in the form of a man, and a most horrendous calamity, danger, and scourge to the people of this place. From what you told me yourselves, it seems that in the matter of her crime all of you owe her a great debt, though you have never shown that you recognized it as such, or even expressed your gratitude. Everything balanced out— things usually do. Why, then, misjudge anybody by invoking the shades of old, bygone things?

The blind man was rude when asking for alms. He cursed, complained, made arrogant demands, beating with his staff on the doors of houses or on shop counters. He was respected, even so; you never saw anyone who ignored him, censured him, or upbraided him, thus relegating him to his properly lowly place. Was it because of pity? Christian charity? More likely they sensed in him a spirit of command, the quality of power. He was called Clubfoot, with no surname or other handle. Exactly like Marmalade Mule: two unfortunates with unfortunate nicknames. Don't you see that by denying them the right of Christian names, you lent to their rebellious poverty an unholy necessity to live apart?

What with Clubfoot's angry, blasphemous demands for alms, nobody delayed a second in giving him money, food, or whatever else he asked for in God's name. "He's a thorough-going rascal!—an impudent, rude piece of riff-raff." But only once in a great while would someone give vent to his feelings in this way, and then only when Clubfoot was a long way off. He was an evil man, with the face of a murderer. A big knife hung outside his rags. He would hold out his large hand in an imperious way

and shout in a voice louder than any dog's bark. If anyone talked, or laughed, he would stop and wait for silence.
He listened very hard to what went on around him; but
he didn't hear everything; that was more than he could
manage.

He was afraid, too; that was something you never suspected. He feared the woman who was his guide. Marmalade Mule would call him by a single syllable, the
"hey" or "hah" almost hissed out from between her teeth;
and Clubfoot would move off, setting his feet in the right
places with her help, the knife swinging from side to
side in its sheath fastened to a string at his waist. He
really got a move on when she called him. They would
go down the street and turn into an alley in each other's
company, those two who were joined in a kind of holy
hatred. Prowling, like a she-wolf and a dog. And what was
the reason for their forming this union of noncommunica-
tion and ill will, when each made the other feel zero at
the bone? Why, blind Clubfoot was the son of her dead
husband, Old Bogey, the man she had killed.

It happened, as you know, a good many years ago. Old
Bogey was infamous for his cruelty: a born criminal,
a man who loved the taste of blood, a monster of iniquity.
He forgave nothing, and he'd just as soon send a man's
soul to the devil as not. He killed, tortured, killed. They
say he made jagged cuts in the bodies of those he knifed,
just for the fun of seeing the faces they made. Can this
have been true? At any rate, in those days he kept everyone a-tremble, without respite or remedy. They said he
was half crazy. He was the scourge of God, that big
hulking demon, that hellhound. And yet he not only got
on well with his wife, they actually loved each other. If

you ask how that was possible, I will simply answer that "love" is the vaguest, most indefinite of words. But I did make inquiries, being an outsider, and learned that Old Bogey really was fond of his wife, Marmalade Mule, though she frightened him, too, in a way. Exactly what kind of fear it was we can only guess. He may have had a presentiment that she was the one person who could destroy him, cut off his mad, evil life with a "No." He may have guessed that his end was already decreed and waiting, ready, in her hands. He loved her and he feared her, too, with the same fear blind Clubfoot was never free of later. The people who answered my questions, however, may have understood nothing of all this; they were simple bearers of a message whose meaning they were ignorant of.

Blind Clubfoot was big and strong. Led by Marmalade Mule, he would come out of the alley erect and without stumbling. People say he drank, but you can see for yourselves that such cock-and-bull stories hide the truth. He did not drink, for the simple reason that Marmalade Mule wouldn't let him. She never had to put her prohibition into words; she had only to let him feel her terrifying silence. And he obeyed her; the mark of the dog collar was on him. He became inured to desires drowned so deeply as to be undecipherable. He feverishly inhaled the spirits of rum at the doors of grogshops, finally going on, treacherously dragging his feet, thoroughly ungrateful, his appetites unsatisfied, gnashing his rat's teeth. He didn't know that he must drink nothing that was not— oh, that it were!—human blood, his thirst and drunkenness being fatal, dangerous to others. That was the reason Marmalade Mule denied him drink. Was he really one of

God's creatures? There's no telling. His flesh may have been molded of different clay from that of other men— ill-sent, sullied, ill-omened. So say the old stories. At any rate, in the shadow state of deprivation in which he felt his way along, barely existing, one thing is clear enough: he was his father's son, a hellhound, too, in plain truth.

If his father, Old Bogey, got along so peaceably with Marmalade Mule, and if she needed him, as poor people do need each other, then why did she kill him? Since you never really thought about her motives, you simply blamed her. But isn't it stupid not to even try to ascertain the truth? When she killed her husband, without any obvious reason that anyone could see, everybody breathed a sigh of relief and thanked God. Now you would be able to live in peace since, by a fortunate chance, this place had been rid of its evil. Old Bogey was the only one who should have been sorry, since he had to go back to hell where he came from. But you didn't thank Marmalade Mule; far from it. You let her suffer ignominy in mute misery because, after all, there was no question about it— she had killed her husband. But then she became terror-stricken, with a deathly fear that she could not withstand. It gripped her vitals and, falling into a cold stupor, she howled like a dog. She began most horribly to not-laugh; and those of you who could not hear her not-laugh as anything but hysterical laughter can, nevertheless, hardly bear to remember the sound.

If I tell you what I know instead of what you believe, it will make you uneasy and you will not like it. You may not even let me finish explaining. The woman had to kill, had to perform with her own hands that deed which was for the common good. Only she could execute that

high task which none of you dared conceive of consciously but which, in your innermost hearts, you prayed
should be done. She, the Mule, had come into the world
destined for the express fate of loving that man and being
loved by him; victim and executioner had been sent
together. Why? Well, all around us are the densest,
blackest shadows—of what is universal. Did Marmalade
Mule and Old Bogey, in the thread-by-thread weaving of
their love, have any inkling of the penalty, the final sentence? He feared her, it was true, and the love he felt
for her placed him at the mercy of her justice. The Mule,
poor woman, suffered perhaps more keenly than anyone
else at her excruciating sacrifice of Old Bogey as agent
for who knows what powers; without being aware of it,
herself suffered for all who are threatened and humiliated, or who weep for their dead. If only she could kill
her man, then she must kill him. Wouldn't she have gone
mad if she had not—if she had refused to satisfy what
every one of you, when alone, pleaded for every single
second? The color of coal is a mystery: people think it is
black—or white.

In my mind's eye I see them coming again down the
indifferent street, and passing by in their rags, completely set apart from the exemplary lives of all the other
inhabitants of this serene village of ours. Clubfoot would
advance, pretending to be quite sure of his footing and
not giving her the end of his staff to hold on to. She was
guiding him solely by the fact that she was in front of
him; the displacement of air her body made let him follow
her as birds fly in formation. Perhaps what he sensed in
front of him was her living essence, her soul's shadow;
or he may have smelled her lupine odor. One noted the

way Clubfoot held his head high from an inexplicable kind of pride; he seemed to have come from some kingdom of the proud, with his spiteful temperament and his startling power to command. He wore a flat hat which was neither white nor black, and you must have noticed how often it fell off his head, especially when he was demanding alms in his most passionate state of large gestures, crudeness, and malice. Did you notice, though, how at these times Marmalade Mule picked up his hat and tried to wipe it clean with her hands before handing it back to him—that hat which he never doffed intentionally because he did not want to show respect to anyone? I know that you really didn't care a copper cent about that woman; you never bothered to observe how she walked, felt, lived, acted. Did you, for instance, ever notice how she looked at the houses with her simple eyes quite free of a beggar's cursed envy? And when she looked at children, her eyes lacked the morose look of bondage which she turned on adults. She looked at everything with innocent admiration. But you could not love her or even tolerate her presence, because you were not aware that an overpowering destiny had singled her out and set her outside human society. By doggedly carrying out her duty, she took on herself all the hate that should have been directed at the two men. When you say she was accursed, was she so, really? At any rate, don't say to me, ever again: "Look out for a wolf in wolf's clothing!" Life itself is the counterweight in the other pan of the scales.

No one knows precisely what the relationship was between these two as they pursued their haphazard, tortuous, monstrous meanderings, like cattle strayed from the path, which you found so funny and made such sport of. Maybe it was all witchcraft and odium, you say, all antipathy and hatred between she-wolf and dog: a calling-up of demons. Or maybe some clandestine super-naturalism, since, of course, there does exist a brother-hood of evil ones, a rabble of the damned, a witches' coven. No, no, there was no hatred; you are quite wrong. There was none on her part, at least. She took care of him, guided him, watched over him as one even more unfor-tunate, more savage, and weaker than herself. She had looked out for him ever since her husband, Old Bogey, had *died*. She assumed his care as a duty from which she sought no surcease. She had no children of her own— "She never whelped . . ." as you say accusingly. You would have been happier, I imagine, if she had just dis-appeared, dead or alive, when she killed her husband. That's how much you hated her.

But if she had killed herself, too, what would Clubfoot have done to you or me? You remember that at that time he was not yet blind and he was every bit as wicked as his father—as ready for cruel and bloody deeds and as ready, too, to deny God. He, too, was of Judas's seed, of that same inhuman, terrible, awesome lineage.

Clubfoot's eyes were still whole then, capable of mirror-ing his inevitable hatred, of fulfilling their role of shoot-ing out rays of venom, of selecting the fattest, tenderest victims. But then, one perfectly ordinary day, Clubfoot was blinded in both eyes. Have you any idea how it hap-pened? Did you ever try to find out? There are potions and powders, you know, which can be made from plants—venoms to steal away sight from eyes that should not see. That's all it was; just that, and there was Clubfoot, stopped in his tracks, a relatively harmless creature who had to renounce his former ways. And you, the worthy inhabitants of the village, now enjoyed security, safe from his unbridled villainies. Now maybe he would not have to die, damned like Old Bogey, his father. I wonder whether Old Bogey would have had to die so, if a certain person had thought *before* of those herbs which blind, or had known how to use them and what effects they would have. If that had happened, then now we would have had Marmalade Mule guiding both of them through the streets, caring for them both out of her terrible love-duty, as if they were the children she had never had, to whom she never gave birth nor ever would; that docile dead man and the thwarted blind one. Her duty would have been to prevent them from doing evil and to give them, as she said in her old-fashioned speech, *shelter and refuge*. But then I guess you were deaf to her muffled voice.

That voice frightened Clubfoot on the rare occasions when he heard it. You know what was so queer about him? That even though he was a blind man, he felt he had to turn his head in order not to see; and that's what he did in order not to face the woman he hated. Blind Clubfoot turned toward the calm, sensible people whom he despised for their peace and harmony. He had to kill if he were to fulfill himself, to be at ease and full of well-being. But his blindness denied him this relief—he could never be at peace. And so blind, mutinous Clubfoot spewed out insults, foamed at the mouth, and howled in his dog's throat. Was it because he knew that he was of another race, had come still unformed from a chaos where he had never been tamed by fear? Blind Clubfoot was frustrated and made impotent by his blindness; he could no longer sink his teeth into someone when his rage consumed him. Isn't that so? Blind Clubfoot muttered to himself, he blasphemed against the unseen. To him, in his blindness, one world was as invisible as the other. But what would things have been like if he could still have seen? Would anyone have dared try to muzzle that mad dog? Despite all this, can you still blame this woman, the Mule, judging her and finding her odious? Couldn't you just leave her in peace if you could understand neither her nor him? Each of us has his depths, just as each has his heights.

Should you have studied her to see how well she knew how to fulfill her obligation, you would have found that she could not be observed; you could never see that. But what you could have seen, at least, if you had looked closely, was that she was incapable of acting rashly; she never failed to pick up any jagged bit of glass she found in the middle of the road, laying it to the side so that it would hurt no one. And she saw such things because she often walked with downcast eyes; perhaps thinking of her husband, the dead man, and of how she had killed him without letting him suffer needlessly. If she had not killed him, mightn't she have damned herself still more irrevocably? As she did with the broken glass, she drew blind Clubfoot away from the wineshop—Clubfoot, the noisy, disorderly disturber of the peace. Their dialogue consisted of a clearing of the throat and a curse. He followed her like a dog. Off they went, but you didn't watch them; we almost never take the trouble to follow the threads that make up a bundle of facts, even when we might be able to do so. They lived in an appalling silence, there together in their burrow. Light shines on all; it is darkness which is different for each of us.

People said that formerly, at least, they were lovers. She, his paramour? You know that's a lie; but all of us love to seize on simpleminded, satisfying theories of that kind. You know perfectly well that she herself patiently led blind Clubfoot, the unruly dog, to the brothel and waited for him outside to make sure the women would not mistreat him. That was, of course, a long time ago, before he grew old and gaunt and got those white hairs which became him so well when his hat fell off so that you could see his grizzled head. All this happened during those years when none of us paid any attention to them. Blind Clubfoot was beginning to stoop then and grow weaker; he grew as lean as a hungry dog. And his fear of Marmalade Mule seemed different, and greater. He no longer had that same fierce, all-consuming fury to live; he was no longer quite so peremptory in demanding his rights— the ferocious right to beg.

It seemed that his fear of her made him whine complaints and plead with Marmalade Mule. And yet she was gentler with him every day, out of pity for his being good for nothing. But he didn't believe she pitied him, could not recognize her feeling for what it was; he trusted neither her nor us. The emotions people feel for one another are usually capricious and exaggerated and come too late. He whispered, as in a dissembling, impersonal way he begged forgiveness; did you notice? But Marmalade Mule always heard him without showing that she did. She tried not to look at him. I know you never noticed any of this. But now you felt a little safer, a little less worried, for it seemed likely that you would soon be rid of what you hated, what so damnably sickened and pursued you.

I was told that he once tried to kill her. It may have been at a time when his fear of her became uncontrollable for some unfathomed reason. He was already in pretty bad shape when he fell sick of a violent fever. He sat down on the curb, gasping for breath. Then, suddenly, he sprang up awkwardly, without the help of his staff, howling and bellowing, as excited as a dog that's been waked up suddenly. He pulled his knife out of its sheath and, stropping it, advanced dementedly, veritably blindly, and in his insane fury tried to strike her. She stayed perfectly still where she was. Is it possible that she was not afraid? She looked off in the direction of nothing. If he had hit the mark by some chance, he'd have cut her to ribbons. But soon he realized that his knife would never find her, and he felt completely forsaken and alone. Fear froze the marrow in every bone in his body. The knife fell from his hand. His fear could find no eyes to fill.

And he groaned and wept: "Mother . . . Mamma . . . oh, Mother!" he implored in a whine as he fell to the ground, his superfluity of fury drained away. He shivered and sat trembling, like meadow grass blown by a wind. He was stuck in the neck of the funnel, sure enough. Marmalade Mule came to him without a word, without a murmur. She picked up his hat, dusted it off, and replaced it on his head, and took his knife and put it back again in its old sheath at his waist. Clubfoot seemed to grow smaller from pain and trembling, shrinking like some wild forest creature. Perhaps she had tears in her eyes; she may have said sadly, with terrible tenderness:

"My son . . ." and she looked beyond him and said something quite different, as if she were speaking to Old Bogey, weeping for that husband whom fate took from her by her own hand. You'd probably rather not know about that; safe in the midst of that devil's chaos, you know nothing. And what good will it do you to hear? No one ever understands anyone else nor will ever understand anything; and that's a fact.

Anyhow, the two of them stayed until nightfall—in fact, until well into the night—in a nearby deserted place on a bank near a fence. Did anyone help them? They say he suffered horribly, unbearably, suffocating from his inability to breathe. There was clearly no hope that he was not dying. He threw himself about in convulsions. None of you saw him draw his last evil breath as dawn broke. No, but you gravely affirm what you imagine is true, that before the night was spent Marmalade Mule had strangled the poor devil to keep him from suffering any longer, and that the marks of her dug-in nails and fingers were found on the neck of the corpse. The only reason she was not accused of murder and arrested was that you were too relieved to see the last of her. And so she went with Clubfoot to his last resting place, as silent as she had always been. Did you despise her even then, at a distance?

Afterward she went away, in bitterness, with no farewells from anyone, stumbling and tired. Without offering her even some grudging bit of charity, you watched her go, sent her off as a scapegoat—in expiation. Ugly, furtive, wolfish, emaciated; you expelled her from your adjudging hearts. But aren't you even going to go out to retrieve her dead body so that you can bury her, all contrition, with wailing and baked funeral meats? It won't be hard to find her where she fell, not a league from here. She was bound a long way off, bound so far, burning, alone and lonely, on her legs so thin for walking, walking. What I am telling you is all true. So never forget, commit to memory, tell your children and your children's children, what you saw with these voraciously fearful eyes of yours and could neither prevent, nor understand, nor forgive. Tell how, just as she left the village, she found, at the end of the street, the carcass of a dead dog, abandoned and already beginning to rot, and slinging it across her bent back, carried it off. Did she do it to free the village of the danger of pestilence? Out of pity, and in order to give the animal burial in the earth? Or so that she might have something to hold in her arms in the hour of her great solitary death? Think about her, meditate on her, meanwhile.

❖ THE ALDACIOUS
NAVIGATOR

IT WAS on the morning of a misty, drizzly day, when nothing much seemed to be happening around the hearth in the open kitchen on the porch behind the little house. It's like that, so nice, in the country. Mamma, still in her robe, told Maria Eva to fry some eggs with cracklings and peel the ripe papayas. Mamma, the loveliest, the best. Pele's slippers would have fitted on her tiny feet. Her hair beamed silent gold. The three little girls, the apples of her eye, were playing with their dolls. Gypsy, Pele, and Imp —all blossoms on one branch. Only Zito was an outsider; he was just a cousin. Rainy midmorning wrapped in tints of green: the fluffy-fluffy sprinkle that makes you a kind of prisoner on the porch or in the house, surrounded by all that mud. You could still see the gully, the chicken yard, the great big crooked cashew tree, a piece of a hill

—and the far distance. Black Nurka was asleep. Mamma watched the three little girls and the boy with long glances full of pride. Especially Imp, the youngest. Because Imp sometimes played tricks.

Not then, though. Imp had installed herself, quicksilver quiet, on top of a crate of potatoes. All crisscross with her legs in an X, she was busy with the box of matches. This is how you saw Imp: first her long, straight, copper-blond hair, and then diminutive things glimpsed within its masses: her not-long face, the sharp little profile, a tiny caressable nose. Gradually she stopped being still and began to flutter like a swallow, peeping out at the shee-shee-shee and the soaking wet landscape—her eyelashes going flicker-flicker. But you couldn't see much, she said, between the rain-strands. "It's raining so hard it'll freeze me!" Then she stretched and kicked up her legs, knocking against various objects with her feet. "Oh, ouch!" rolling in the hands of bananas, with her navel showing. Pele helped her straighten herself out. ". . . And the cashew tree still makes flowers," she added, noticing that the tree's work was never interrupted even by days and days of raininess, the foggy drizzle and the pale morning in the sky. Mamma was measuring out sugar and flour for a cake. Diligentle Pele tried to help. Gypsy was reading a book; she did not have to turn the pages when she read.

Gypsy and Zito stayed a little apart from each other, not being on very good terms since a big, ugly quarrel the day before. Pele was the brunette of the family, with remarkable eyes. Gypsy was a pretty girl if there ever was one: a portrait in miniature of Mamma. Zito mumbled over thoughts he did not dare express, jealous thoughts; he had given way to jealousy, of what or of whom he did not know. Imp sprang up in a pirouette. "I know why an egg's like a skewer!"—she was always concocting riddles. But she wouldn't tell the answer to a soul. That's the way Imp was: not touched in the head, but full of secrets. And infinitesimal worries: "My head's hot today"—when she didn't want to study. And then: "I'm going to learn geography." Or: "I wish I knew about love . . ." It was Pele who burst out laughing. Gypsy and Zito raised their eyes, startled. They nearly, nearly looked at each other, their eyes not quite meeting. Gypsy, who was sure she was right, was pouting. But Zito did not want to be angry any longer; he could hardly stand it. When he eyed Gypsy on the sly, she all at once looked even prettier, and ready to fly away.

"If you don't know about love, can you read grown-up novels?" speculated Imp. "Hmmm? You can't even read your catechism." Pele flicked her sister with just a light touch of scorn; but Pele was never unkind and only pinched gently; there was always a smile in her voice. Imp, piqued, quipped: "Smarty! I read all thirty-five words on the matchbox label, so there." She loved to make nonsensical little pronouncements in a superior tone and with great vigor of expression: "Zito, is a shark *hallucinated?* or *explicit?* or a *demagogue?*" Maker of poetry that she was, she loved to drag in those serious words which light up long clearings in the darkness of our ignorance. Zito did not answer: all at once he felt desperate and quarrelsomely culpable. He longed to take his leave theatrically, under the rainy rain; he was bursting with anger. But Imp

had the gift of apprehending tenuous, shadowy things
and appropriating and reflecting them in herself—the
thingness of things and the peopleness of people. "Zito,
couldn't you be the inglorious pirate sailor in an unimpaired ship, sailing far, fa-a-ar away, the navigator nevermore, for everyone?" Zito smiled with a resolute air.
Gypsy started, held the book with both hands, hesitated.
Mamma gave Pele the bowl to beat the eggs in.

But Imp rested her face on her hand, caught up now in
her tale, giving way to the flood of storytelling: "The
Aldacious Navigator, the valetudinarian, sailed off to discover new lands. He sailed in a fraudulent ship, too. All
alone. Those places were a long way off on the ocean. The
Aldacious Navigator missed his mother, and his brothers
and sisters, and his father. But he didn't cry. He respec-
tively had to go. He said: 'Will you really forget me?' The
day came when his ship was ready to go. The Aldacious
Navigator didn't turn his back on the people left behind.
And the people still waved their white handkerchiefs.
Finally there was no more ship to see, only the rest of the
ocean. Then one of them thought and said: 'He's going
to discover places we'll never find. . . .' Then—and then
another one said: 'He'll discover all those places, and then
he'll never come back again.' And then another one
thought and thought, circumferentially, and said: 'Then
he must be mad at us inside, without knowing it.' Then
they all cried very hard and went sadly back home to
supper."

Pele lifted the spoon: "You're an 'aldacious' little silly."
"And you're a false hypocrite," Imp cried rudely. "Why did
you make up that silly story, dopey, dopey?" Gypsy said
angrily, because she was hurt. "Because it may have a

happy ending, that's why!" Nurka barked. Was Mamma mad too, because Imp had knocked over the coffeepot and some other things with her foot? Then Imp said reflectively: "It's better to talk through your hat than keep foolishness under it. . . ." Then she closed her green eyes, solemnly repentant for her rambunctious behavior. She probably heard nothing but the sizzling rain that sounded like something frying.

The morning was a sponge. But Pele must have said ten prayers to St. Anthony while she was beating the eggs, for a miracle blossomed softly. The weather began to clear, though it was still only March, with its usual rains. Gypsy and Zito sighed at each other. The hens were let out of the chicken coop and the turkey turned loose. Nurka bounded off. Could the sky actually be turning blue?

Mamma was going to visit a sick woman, the wife of the tenant farmer Zé Pavio. "Oh, are you going without us or within us?" asked Imp. Mamma, so as not to laugh nor yet to ignore her, chaffed her gently: "What a crazy little girl!" Hers was a voice of sweet open vowels. The morning turned flowery. The children asked permission to go and see the brook overflowing its banks. Mamma gave her consent; they weren't little apron-string girls any more. They burst into rejoicing. But someone would have to go along to see that they didn't forget and go too near the dangerous water. The stream there was very high. And wasn't Zito the very person to go with them, already half a man, trustworthy and responsible? The gloom had lifted from the air. But they had to put on warmer clothes. "Oh, the bubbly bubbles!" Imp was merrier than any of them, joyful as if, if, if: a little girl who was more like a bird. "Go with God," said Mamma oracularly, in her lilting voice. When she spoke, a gush of blessings rained onto them. The little family separated.

The path they had to follow to get to where they were going first climbed subvexly up the steep little knoll. The two umbrellas followed it. Under one—in front—Imp and Pele. Under the other, Zito and Gypsy. There was only some leftover rain, a murmuring drizzle. Nurka ran blackly and then doubled back, an unbottled, happy dog. If you turned around you could see the little white house with a blue-green stripe, the smallest and prettiest of all, of all. Zito gave Gypsy his arm; sometimes, often, their hands met. Pele seemed taller, elegant. Agile little Imp, in her coleopterous jacket, walked with her toes turned in like an intrepid little parakeet.

As they crossed the hill, Zito and Gypsy kept an awkward silence full of feeling. Yes, they had made up now and were trying out their happiness; for them the outing was a matter of emotion. Now they were going down the other side of the little hill, very carefully because it was slippery and there were mud puddles, but also so as not to step in what Imp called "the bovine"—tall cylinders of mushroom-covered dung. Cows often did pass there— "cowardly cows"; and Imp fell down. She said that Mamma had told them to be brave and sensible. But that was a fib. And then: "Well, now I've got myself dirty, so I cannot be careful any more." She ran down the lower slope with Nurka in the green, green grass. Pele scolded her: "Are you going to look for an audacious navigator?" But there was more to it than that. Meanwhile, in the wetness, in the light, the flat grassland bloomed: daisies bewilderingly mingled, their centers surrounded by fluttering eyelids.

The place they wanted to get to was the little cove where the creek makes a delta. Below it, in the clumped bamboos and the gravel pit at the edge of the river, they heard the water snorting and whoofling. Because the river was growing rough and boisterous, so was the creek, its estuary too full of refuse, dammed up, crested with wavelets—it roared like a great bore. "Old wind puffer!" Imp shouted at it. Its last bit of sand disappeared under a dancing tablecloth of foam, the boiling bubbles beautifully random. Imp looked and learned it all by heart. She thrust in bamboo wands, marking places to measure the water as it rose. But its seething reminded her of other things. Imp did not like the sea: "It doesn't have a pattern. The wind won't let it. It's too big. . . ." She wished she had brought bread for the fishes. "Fish, on a day like this!" Pele was doubtful. Imp's thoughts wandered off again. "The waterfall is a little wall of water. . . ." She said the island in the river there in front of them was the Isle of the Alligators. "Did you ever see any alligators there?" teased Pele. "No, but you never saw an alligator not be there either. All you can see is the island. So the alligator might be there or he might not." But Imp, with Nurka at her side, had already seen, with her two bird's eyes, everything that was visible from where she stood. Making a thousand and one superfluous movements, the water was gradually rising and growing wider.

They sat down nearby, not on the ground or on fallen tree trunks because they were rainy and wet. On a stone just big enough for two, Gypsy and Zito could have sat for hours, talking desultorily as banal people do. Pele had gone off to pick a bunch of flowers. It was not drizzling any more. Imp was jumping up and down again. She said that the day was very recitable. Going back to the bank, the greenest possible bank, she began to throw stones as far as she could for Nurka to fetch. Then she crouched down for a change; it looked as if she had on only one shoe. But then, without getting up, she spun around on her tiny feet, wanting Gypsy and Zito to listen to her. She stared at them.

"The Aldacious Navigator didn't like the sea! But he had to go anyway. He loved a girl, a thin girl. But when the wind blew, the sea came up and took his boat with him inside it, scrutinizing. The Aldacious Navigator couldn't do a thing about it; there was only the darned preliminary ocean all around him. The Aldacious Navigator thought about the girl all the time. Love is original. . . ."

Gypsy and Zito smiled and laughed at the same time. "For goodness' sake! Are you still on that subject?" It was Pele, back with a great heap of flowers which she held like a shield. Imp pantomimed a "hah!" and stubbornly went on with her tale: ". . . The crew came . . . no, not yet. And then it rained and rained. The sea filled up, it was an instructive scheme. . . . There was nowhere for the Aldacious Navigator to run and hide, and the ship was falling to pieces. The ship was parabulating. . . . He was so scared he hardly had time to think about the girl he was circumspectly in love with. He was just prevaricating. . . . Love is singular. . . ."

"And then?"

"The girl was parallel, away far off, all alone, she had

to stay there; really, the two of them were on the two tips of homesickness. . . . Love, that is . . . the Aldacious Navigator was in total, titular danger . . . there was no hope. . . . The Aldacious . . . the Aldacious . . ."

"Yes. All right. And then what?" Pele challenged her.

"Then what? Then . . . and then . . . I'll explain it! All right. Then he turned on the ocean light. That was it. He had made an arrangement with the lighthouse man. . . . That's what he did. And . . ."

"Unh-unh, that doesn't count! You can't make up a new character at the end of the story. Phooey! And—look at your Aldacious Navigator. There he is."

They looked. It was he: a sizable lump of cow dung, partly dried, a bucolic offering on the slimy ground at the edge of the grass—flat, abandoned. On its little eminence had sprouted a mushroom with a thin, flexible stalk, quite long: the little white hat above it swayed pertly. The edge of the floodwater was almost upon it.

Imp made a face. But just then Pele's bouquet came undone and a few flowers fell to the ground. "Oh! Yes it is, it really is!"—and Imp leaped into action, swift to take advantage of any opportunity. She caught up the little yellow flowers—Johnny-jump-ups, goldenrod, and daisies —and stuck them into the crusted crown of the object. "Aren't there any blue flowers today?" she asked. Everyone laughed in unison, and Gypsy and Zito clapped their hands. "Now then. It's the Aldacious Navigator"—and Imp stuck him full of things: bamboo leaves, little branches, twigs. The "bovine" was being transfigured.

Just then they heard a faraway rumble: thunder dragging its furniture. Imp was terribly afraid of thunder. She drew closer to Gypsy and Zito. And to Pele. Gentle Pele, who asked: "Well? Isn't there any more story? Is that all?"

"Well, all right, I'll begin again. The Aldacious Navigator was in love with the girl all over again. So . . . all of a sudden he was ashamed of being scared, he grew brave and wasn't afraid any longer. He gave an omnipotent leap. . . . From afar off he grabbed the girl and hugged her. . . . That's what he did. It was the ocean that was dumfounded. Oh, heck! The Aldacious Navigator, that's the whole tale. Now it's really finished: I've written 'The End'!"

The water had almost reached the Aldacious Navigator; the first wave to come along would bump it. "Will he go so sea?" asked Imp anxiously. She was standing very straight. A light breeze tickled her, patted her face, her lips, yes, and her ears and hair. The rain, far off, was postponed.

Whispering and looking thoughtfully at each other, Gypsy and Zito were poised on the edge of reality. "It's so nice today, isn't it? Everything, all of us getting along so well, everyone happy. . . . I like this weather." And: "So do I, Zito. Are you going to come back often?" And: "I sure will if I can." And: "Zito, could you do what the Aldacious Navigator did? Go discover other lands?" And: "Maybe he went because the other lands are even nicer. . . ." And so the two of them said big things in little words, you to me, I to you, and so on. For all that they were so happy, something else struggled confusedly inside them—rose-love-thorns-heartache.

But now the water rushed up to the Aldacious Navigator, to and fro and away, the spume surrounding it and beginning to drench it. Behold the Aldacious Navigator, circumnavigable though still on terra firma; the soil still kept it from breaking away entirely. Imp added still more adornments. Even Gypsy and Zito lent a hand. And Pele. Now the object was completely transformed—highly colored, extravagant, decked with leaves and flowers. "He's going off to discover new lands." "No, Imp. Don't make fun of serious things." "Well for heaven's sake! Why not?" Then Gypsy pensively proposed: "Shall we send a message with him?" Send something out to sea? They all wanted to. Zito added a coin. Gypsy a hairpin. Pele a piece of chewing gum. Imp—a spitball: that was her style. And what about the story? Would there still be time to tell the real, true story? Well—

"Now I know. The Aldacious Navigator didn't go by himself: so there! He sailed with the girl that they were in love and they went on board the ship, strictly. That's it. The ocean carried them aesthetically along. They went in the ship without being alone, and the ship was nicer and nicer, the ship . . . That's what it was. And it turned into fireflies."

That's what it was. A terrible thunderclap filled heaven and earth, unconquerable. The sky grew overcast. Imp and the thunder were both choked off. Would she fall into an "unimpaired" abyss—the void of the thunder? Nurka came barking to her aid. Gypsy, Pele, and Zito, too, ran to protect her. But just then a fairy figure appeared unexpectedly against the flowers.

"Mamma!"

Imp flung her arms around her mother's neck. Mamma

stroked the little girl's head, as if she were a squirrel holding a nut. Imp laughed without flickering her eyelashes.
And Pele cried:

"Look! Right this minute! There goes the Aldacious
Navigator!"

"Hey!"

"Oh!"

Aldacious! He was off. Bobbing, dipdancing, foamy
waters bearing him away, the Aldacious Navigator wandered off downstream forever, with his leafy branches, his
flowers, and the long, dignified, graceful mushroom with
its dewdrop—one glistening little drop—at the very pin-
nacle of a lump of dried cow shit.

Imp's heart was touched. Then, recovering herself, she
said: "Mamma, now I know something else: the only
thing like an egg is a skewer!"

The rain came down again in torrents.

And the umbrellas opened their wings.

● **HONEYMOONS**

JUST WHEN THINGS are at their samiest sameness, something new turns up. I had felt sort of weak and lazy the day before; could I be going into a kind of no-account nothing? It was around the first of November, I remember. Now, I'm a peace-loving man, as far as people let me be, not a bit like what I was when I was a young blade: then it was all rakehell, rebellion, and devil-take-the-hindmost. But later it was real life, all right, and a damned hard one. I'm a pretty good rancher—that is, I'm not dirt poor, and I'm not filthy rich, either. Self-defense and caution are two things that are never in short supply at Holy Cross of the Wildcat, this ranch where everybody's welcome, my ranch, a real haven. I was so fagged out from the heat that day that I couldn't move anything but my eyeballs. That day was sure nothing times nothing. I was bored and grumpy, so I ate too much, and after lunch I packed myself off to the hammock in my bedroom. It was a matter of age, digestion, and general health: liverish, I was feeling. My wife, Sa-Maria Andreza, who's a good soul but a little past her prime, had gone off to boil a cup of tea to settle my overloaded stomach. Good. Seo Fifino, my son, who was sitting outside, told me that a fellow who was acting as a messenger had come with a letter. I didn't do anything for a while. Hustle and bustle aren't my style.

As that son of mine, Seo Fifino, who wasn't any fool or any rascal, either, told the story, that fellow had snuck up so quiet-like that nobody had noticed him until he tied his horse behind the well: the dogs hadn't barked, the gate hadn't creaked. He was well armed, too, with an automatic rifle slung over his shoulder. And just about then my overseer, Satisfied Joe, whispered his name to me: Baldualdo. Well, there I sat, a mosquito on a wildcat's jaw: didn't bat an eyelash, didn't turn a hair. I knew Baldualdo's reputation—he could whip a whole posse by himself, and most of his customers were dead. Now I'm not one to gossip. I will say this, though: my Satisfied Joe, also known as Zé Sipío, had his hand on his gunstock; you get what I mean—I recalled the days when us ranchers were in a shooting war with Major Lidelfonso and his men. I was with him and so were a lot of other good men. Life's got a lot of rough places in it; if you set the table, you eat the meat. I hauled myself out of the hammock and went to take a squint at my visitor. He gave me a quick look, sized me up, and asked me to tell him again what my whole name was. The letter he had for me was important all right. I looked at the signature three times: Seo Seotaziano.

Well, what do you know about that? Here's what I spelled out: "My esteemed friend and comrade . . ." From his ranch house, way off, Seo Seotaziano handled all his important business with a short fuse and a long arm. A real leader. People kept their distance because he was half tiger, half lion, and all wildcat, but fair and square and as good as fresh bread. He was one of the right kind. He was my best friend from way back, and the only man I'd ever taken orders from. And believe me, that was a long time ago. But now he had remembered me, taking my loyalty for granted. He had a problem. He might be exaggerating; however you looked at it, there was sure to be dogs, cats, and commotion. I'd have to back him up and believe me, I'd do it willingly. Where he scratched a line, I'd cut deep.

The gist of the letter was this: "I'm asking you to take a young man and a girl under your protection. We'll see to the rest when the time comes." What craziness love gets people into! I had to smile. My liver was back to scratch, and I began getting ready.

Quietly, quietly, I did what had to be done—accommodating those visitors we were expecting; seeing that nothing interfered. Giving necessary orders for a light supper to be got ready. A man forewarned is worth four men armed. That was a Saturday. I came to an understanding with Satisfied Joe and my boy, Seo Fifino; they were to bring in certain men from the middle farm and a couple from Munho's farms. Some workers were to stay where they were that day to do the chores, but I wanted

those I'd picked to be handy: they were resourceful men,
if I needed them. We had plenty of rice and beans, and
charges of gunpowder, lead and bullets. All very sensible,
if I do say so. At peace with God. Calm and careful. Sensible, sincere and honorable.

My wife, Sa-Maria Andreza, was looking at me.

That good fellow, Baldualdo: "If you want me to, sir,
I'll stay on here for a few days . . ." was all he said to me
in a low voice, knowing his job by heart. He was already
my pal—I had my guardian angels to thank for that. I
paced up and down the veranda a few times in soldierly
style. What about the couple that was coming, the boy
and the girl? Sa-Maria Andreza—you could always count
on her to do things right—had prepared one or two bedrooms, with towels, comforts, vases of flowers. They
would almost surely arrive that night, so I said, pretty
shrewdly: "Well, old woman, I guess we'll be playing
fiddles"—joking, as I cleaned the lamp. My helpmate
Sa-Maria Andreza just said, fanning her topknot: "A
scaly-barked pepper tree won't ever be smooth." I gave her
hand a little squeeze. I went over all my weapons again in
my mind. Alackaday, my youth was a long way behind
me.

Sure enough, to nobody's surprise, they came about
midnight. Sweethearts, terribly in love. She was one of
those good-looking girls who catch everybody's eye. I
didn't have a notion what family she came from. A little
bit scared, but with a smile peeking out. And the boy? A
real fine one! One of the best. I saw that right away. He
had a long rifle. Carried himself smart as a soldier. No,
they weren't married yet. They ate supper. Hardly said a
word. The girl went to bed in a room in the very middle of

the house; a real proper young girl. The boy, that brave fellow, wanted to bed down in the sugar mill. A powerful, well-muscled boy. I liked that. I felt I had the right to treat him like a father. Oh, and another thing—they'd come here all by themselves; really eloped. And that made me like them even more. Then, about an hour later, a little more or a little less, another tough came along, a fellow who'd followed a good way behind to keep an eye on them without their knowing it. That was at Seo Seotaziano's orders.

Everything had been done just right, nothing too much, nothing too little, the way nobody but a real leader could plan it. The last fellow was named Bibião, and he was as full of fight as the barrel of a rifle. He asked for my blessing. Good. All set, everything in order, I dozed off, with a right to sweet dreams. Why not? My men were already off, and they'd be in the saddle all night. One was going straight to Hollyhock Ranch, my old compadre Veríssimo's place, to borrow three rifles, three men. Just to be on the safe side. In a fight those fellows blaze up like hot coals. My other men had gone to Horse Lake to get another three, so my compadre Serejério wouldn't feel left out. Good. I figure other men are like me. Thinking things out, that's what it takes to be respected; honor, tranquillity, and profit. When everything's on the right track, I sleep sound. The abovementioned philosophy is the one I live by.

I was awake before sunup. Everything was peaceful on my place, lying there covered with dew. I love to look at those things you can always count on, country things, beautiful, sweet-smelling; and not another thing happening. Sa-Maria Andreza came to attend me. I said to her: "Don't let on to me who that girl is or anything she may

have told you." To be on the safe side, I wanted not to
know just then: she might be the daughter of someone I
knew, some relative of mine or a friend. Not that it would
have made any difference. At that time, all loyalty, I was
Seo Seotaziano himself. Nothing less. A hero when it
hurts!—there's a good saying. That day was a Sunday. In
spite of everything, lunch went into hungry mouths. The
girl and the boy gazed at each other right there in front
of me, happy at being so lucky. So many things in this
world do turn out well. Sa-Maria Andreza, my well-pre-
served wife, took enormous trouble with the meal. I
wasn't the only one who thought so; everyone's appetite
spoke for it. That young couple's love affair was like my
own courting days all over again.

We stirred around, nothing bothering us, while the
hours went by as if time stood still. And so that day passed
in clubs and diamonds—and still nothing happened. The
pretty girl said her prayers in the chapel. Sa-Maria Andreza treated her with sincere womanly affection. We men
stayed outside. Seo Fifino, my boy, on this side of the
house; Bibião on the hill, Baldualdo on the bridge over the
stream. There were other men too, lots of them; hidden
away so cleverly you wouldn't have guessed they were
there. With me were Satisfied Joe and the bridegroom,
who didn't have much to say for himself. We strolled
from gully to ditch, inspecting things. Was my own Sa-
Maria Andreza praying for *me*? No, I always exaggerate.
I didn't waste time thinking; I got things done. It was a
day and then some. God be praised. Then evening came,
and the stars we had been waiting for. Then the men
from Hollyhock Ranch and Horse Lake came up in spurts,

a few at a time. They were armed to the fingernails and they weren't smiling. Ah, there's nothing like good friends.

So there were more of us the second night, and the next morning we got up before the roosters again. Then it was doubtful Monday—a round sort of day. A day with lots of company. First came two more men from Seo Seotaziano's ranch. A real leader, Seo Seotaziano. After that came another pair on horseback: the sexton riding a short distance behind the priest. I had sent word for them to come. The priest was a young man; it looked as if he had a shotgun slung on his back. I could see the tip of a knife, and a short-barreled rifle, too. He jumped off his horse and blessed everything in sight, in a hurry for the marrying he had to do: there was going to be a wedding in my house. I had to get a move on and spruce myself up; put on my best clothes for those special few minutes. Sa-Maria Andreza, my wife, arranged the altar so that it looked real pretty. Boy and girl paraded their pride. Love and nothing but love. Hardly touching the earth. The two of them arm in arm. Look what real love can do! Everything good, really good. My Sa-Maria Andreza, all dressed in her best, colored up a little, I think. I'm at my best when the fiddles are going. The priest spoke fine words. By this time I knew who the bride's family was. She was a daughter of Major João Dioclécio, a hard rich man, strong for a fact. A chilly sort of fact . . . Well. I shrugged my shoulders. When I stake out a field I plow it; twisted paths sometimes turn straight. After the wedding was over we went straight from the altar to the table.

It was a banquet of good plain food: suckling pig, turkey and all the fixings, manioc flour, which we always

serve, and several kinds of wine. All of us sat down together, and the priest ate as much as anybody. I had a
good appetite myself, and I didn't feel stuffed when I
stopped. We ended up with dessert and sang some rounds.
The groom had his gun at his belt. The bride was a beautiful thing to see, with her proper veil and wreath. Wool
gets dirtier the longer you use it . . . I thought, seeing
myself just that way. How wonderful to be in love! I
sighed just thinking about it. I went all the way down
from that green valley to the top of that steep hill we all
have to climb. Before the ceremony was over, my brother
João Norberto arrived from his far-off ranch, The Bell-
birds. The news had reached him and he had come to
offer me his help. He had a big piece of news himself. If
the Major attacked with his killers, Seo Seotaziano would
come onto the scene at the head of a hundred men: come
up behind them! That was glorious; I whistled in my
chair. That nice young bridegroom was kin to Seo Seotaziano. Some of my men played the guitar. Shall we dance?

I looked at my healthy Sa-Maria Andreza—betrothed
and bestowed on me.

And that was a night to remember! My pals Serejério
and Veríssimo came in person. They were the kind to
finish what they started. Even the priest said he'd stay, to
confess anyone who needed it when the time came. The
prayerbook lay on the table, with the pistol right alongside. A good priest, an upstanding man, and Seo Seotaziano's friend. Now we were waiting for Major Dioclécio
and his band of varmints. "Tonight for sure!" we said.
"For that kind of business, just wait till it gets dark!"
Someone else said: "Who's going to blow out the candle?"
Here and everywhere, you might say, were patrols,

trenches, and sentinels. Quiet, soft footsteps, rifles clink-
ing. Ah, this old Holy Cross of the Wildcats Ranch has
enough thorns for every mouth and gullet. The point is
that I was the leader. I was already smelling blood; I was
flying high, the way I really am. I myself—in my name
and Seo Seotaziano's.

We had to make a night of it. In the parlor. On these
benches and chairs. By the light of these lanterns and
lamps. All of us who were in command were here. That
is, myself, my brother João Norberto, and our pals Veríssimo and Serejério, and the bridegroom, plus Seo Fifino.
And the bride in her white dress, and Sa-Maria Andreza,
my own wedded wife. The women and the men—a heap
of good men. My Zé Sipío close beside me. Supper—bury-
ing the dinner bones—was lively. Men ate standing up
with their plates in their hands, pricking up their ears.
We were in a fighting good humor and ready for anything.
Let the enemy come!—and damn the Diocletians. It was
time to hold our breath. Here we were waiting, with
enough light to attract a thousand moths. And let's have
the tri-o-li-o-la . . . let's play catch, you might say. What
if no one came? What's this? What's that? What about
it? What's up? Anyway, we were ready.

There we were, one step from death, brave and together, so many, enough. Nobody came. The bride, all
fluffy and fluttery, smiled at the groom; oh, those nuptial
smiles! And my mind was on the wrong thing; I was thinking like a man with a gun. What might be skimpy for
anyone else is more than enough for me. My Sa-Maria
Andreza was smiling at me. That's something old folks
can't have any more: secrets and whispering. Nobody
came. Almost day, and the cocks beginning to crow. The

priest prayed like a warrior, with a fearless delight in his weapons. I felt I was worth something, as I was in my prime. On that happy day I felt nature welling up in me: the dry fountain gushing forth again, the young shoot budding for the second time. Sa-Maria my Andreza looked at me lovingly; she was beautiful and young again. Was no one coming that night? So far, nothing! Daybreak. The bridegroom went off with the bride; and some of the others who were so sleepy they were already snoring in the straw. We decided to take turns keeping watch. I beamed at my Sa-Maria Andreza; on fire with love, God be praised. My hand in hers, I said to her—the rifle in my other hand—"We'll go to sleep in each other's arms." The things that happen at dawn are confided first to the dark. Well. We went to sleep.

I got up later than usual, born again from the cozy, cuddly warmth. Everyone to his post. Now it was Tuesday. Would this be the day? We waited. Half cautious, half jolly but serious too, not making a racket. Well, then? Long-drawn-out calm. And so.

Then came the news: a message. The fellow who brought it was one of Dioclécio's servants: one of his masters was coming today, all by himself, to pay me a visit on his way to somewhere else. A friendly visit. Well, how about that? What now? I went into a huddle with my chief followers to hear what they thought about it, you know. We came to an agreement: that they, with most of the men and the rifles, would go out for a while and wait at the middle farm, which was no more than half a league off. My brother João and my two compadres would go, with the sexton following behind the priest. That would leave the ranch house unguarded. Yes, yes.

Good. So as not to stir up ill feeling, which I always try
not to do. The man was coming alone, wasn't he, as an
ambassador, just to say ahem-ahem? Would he make
threats, complain, try to scare me, declare war on me?
He might do any of those things. My door faces the sunrise. I don't see in any other direction. I'm a very frank
man. I am what I am—myself—Joaquim Norberto. Seo
Seotaziano's friend.

I welcomed the man here, in this doorway to what is
mine. He was a brother of the bride and an acquaintance
of mine, a cordial man with a hearty handshake. We
went in. We sat down. I was calm and serious; he seemed
to feel at home and be in his right mind. He hadn't
come to stir up trouble or make any fuss; he handled himself well. Could the business be settled on friendly terms?
My duty and pleasure is to reconcile, to smooth things over
and put them back together, as an honest man and a
leader of armed men. Now it was time to unsnarl all the
knots on both sides. I let my face clear. I invited the fellow to lunch. And then I made myself plain; when you
just stammer and beat around the barnyard, nothing is
added and nothing is taken away. I called the newlyweds
to the table!

They stood firm—a good brave pair. They came. My
visitor smiled, gave his hand to her and to him, and said:
"How're you? And how're you?"—frank and friendly.
Good. We ate and talked about different things. Good.
Everything was going smoothly, with the grain of the
wood. Speaking softly and hesitating a little, he invited
the couple to go with him: for her parents' blessing and
a back-from-their-honeymoon feast. Wasn't everything all
clear and everybody satisfied now? So he knew about the

wedding. I was invited too, and Sa-Maria darling Andreza. Good, that was the right thing to do, you know. I couldn't just go off, the way things stood. But I sent my son Seo Fifino to represent me. He was glad to go, already looking forward to the party.

The bride and groom were happy to accept the invitation, and after thanking me took their leave. And I answered straight from the heart and straight from the shoulder: "All I want to add is: under God, there's only Seo Seotaziano!" I said. The man stood up to go. And looking right at him, just to make sure—my rule for living right—"I was godfather to those two at their wedding, and I'll be godfather to their first child if they'll let me!" I roared, pretending an open laugh. You never could tell. And he got the point, all right. Not much doubt about that. In this world you'd better say what you mean and put your mark on it. The rifles can take care of the rest.

Sa-Maria Andreza and I watched them from the veranda, riding off on their horses in peace and harmony. It was all finished so suddenly, you might say, no more obligation. No war, no more honeymoons, no more party.

I looked at my Sa-Maria Andreza, who was looking at me. Oh, my. And nothing happened.

Baldualdo and Bibião went away too. There was nothing else for them to do here, you might say. Seo Seotaziano had been served and my duty was done. My overseer, Satisfied Joe, was reluctantly closing the gate. Those honeymoons of ours were over so soon; they hadn't lasted any longer than you could blow on a mouth organ. All that was left were small consolations: make-believe loving, my own little basket to carry water in. What we had to do now was forget our disappointments and start getting old. But someday Seo Fifino, my son, was going to carry off a girl like that—by force of arms! I, Joaquim Norberto, smiled, out of respect for my son, I hugged my Sa-Maria Andreza; our eyes were unclouded, you might say. Well, anyway. Here on Holy Cross of the Wildcats Ranch we keep ourselves company. Oh, well. That's the way it was.

✸ A YOUNG MAN,
GLEAMING, WHITE

ON THE NIGHT of November 11, 1872, in the district of
Sêrro Frio in Minas Gerais, there occurred eerie phenomena which were referred to in contemporary news-
papers and registered in the astronomical tables. According
to these accounts, a glowing missile hurtled out of
space, accompanied by booming blasts. The earth rocked
in a quake that shook the mountain heights, made rubble
of houses, and caused the valleys to tremble. Countless
people were killed. The torrential rainstorm that followed
caused greater floods than any ever seen before; the water
in the streams and rivers rose sixty feet above its normal
level. After this cataclysm the features of the country for
a league around were entirely changed; all that was left
were the wrecks of hills, caves newly blasted open, creeks
shifted from their courses, forests uprooted, new moun-

tains and cliffs upthrust, farms swallowed up without a trace—strewn rocks covering what had been fields. Even some distance away from the monstrous happenings, many men and animals perished by being buried alive or drowned. Others wandered at random, going wherever it pleased God to send them, in their confusion at no longer finding the old roads they knew.

A week later, on the day of St. Felix the Confessor, one of these poor fugitives, who had doubtless been driven from his home by hunger or shock, appeared in the courtyard of Hilário Cordeiro's Casco Ranch. Suddenly he was there, a youth with the appearance of a gentleman but in a pitiable state. Without even rags to cover his nakedness, he had wrapped himself in a thick cloth like a horse blanket, which he had found God knows where. Bashfully, he showed himself there in the early morning light and then disappeared behind the fence of the cow pasture. He was of an amazing whiteness, not at all sickly or wan, but of a fine paleness, semi-gilded with light, which caused him to gleam as if he had a source of brightness inside his body. He seemed to be a foreigner of some kind never met with before in those parts, almost as if he constituted a new race all by himself. They talk about him to this day, though with a good deal of confusion and uncertainty because it was so long ago. The story is told by the children and grandchildren of men who were adolescents, or perhaps even children, when they were fortunate enough to know him.

Because Hilário Cordeiro, a good, God-fearing man, was generous to the poor, more especially in those first days after the catastrophe in which his own relatives had died or suffered total ruin, he unhesitatingly offered the youth

hospitality and thoughtfully provided him with clothing
and food. The stranger was in dire need of such help, for,
as a result of the extraordinary misfortunes and terrors
that he had suffered, he had completely lost his memory
and even his use of speech. In his condition perhaps the
future was indistinguishable from the past: since he had
lost all sense of time and could understand nothing, he
answered neither yea nor nay. His was a truly pitiful
state. He seemed not even to try to understand gestures,
or at any rate often interpreted them to mean the opposite
of what was intended. Since he was bound to have a given
name already, he could not just be given some made-up
one; but no one had any idea what his Christian name was
any more than the surname he must have inherited from
his unknown progenitors. He seemed to be the Son of No
Man.

For days after his arrival the neighbors came to inspect
him. Stupid they certainly did not find him, but he was
subject to a kind of dreamy disinvolvement, tinged by sadness. They were surprised, though, at how unobtrusively
observant he could be—noting every little characteristic
of people and of things. This odd combination of careful
scrutiny and misinterpretation only began to be understood later on. Nevertheless, they all liked him. And the
person who was perhaps most attached to him was the
Negro José Kakende, who was a bit odd himself. This
former slave of a halfwitted musician had been touched
in the head ever since a shock he had suffered during the
calamities in the county, so that he began to wander from
place to place, shouting warnings to the people and crying out wild lunatic tales about a portentous apparition
that he swore he had seen on the banks of the Rio do Peixe

just before the cataclysm. Only one person had a grudge
against the youth from the beginning, and that was a certain Duarte Dias, the father of a beautiful girl named
Viviana. He swore the youth was a rascal, a secret criminal, who, in better times, would have been banished to
Africa or put in irons and thrown into the king's dungeon.
But because he was known to be a hot-tempered, over-
bearing man, and malignant and unjust besides, with a
heart of pure adamant, nobody paid much attention to
him.

One particular day they took the youth to mass, and
though he gave no sign of being a believer or an unbe-
liever, he did nothing untoward. He listened to the singing
and the choral music, seriously and with considerable
feeling. He was not sad exactly, but it seemed as if he felt
a greater nostalgia than other people, a deeper yearning.
Perhaps because he understood nothing of the service, his
feeling was refined into a purer ecstasy—the heart of a
dog who hears his master. His smile, which was more a
matter of the lips than of the eyes and which was never
broad enough to reveal his teeth, sometimes lingered on
his face for long periods, as if he were thinking of some
other place, some other time. After mass, when Father
Bayão gave a kindly talk to the youth, he prefaced it by
unexpectedly making the sign of the cross over him but
found that the young man was not made at all uneasy by
the holy gesture. It seemed to the priest that he floated a
little above the earth, held there by some inner buoyancy
denied to the earthbound. "Compared to him, all of us
ordinary mortals have hard expressions, an ugly look of
habitual weariness." These lines were written by the priest
in a letter which he signed and sealed as a witness of the

coming of the exquisitely strange wanderer and sent to
Canon Lessa Cadaval of the Mariana See. In this letter he
also mentioned the Negro José Kakende, who had ap-
proached him on the same occasion with loud and extravagant accounts of the vision he had had at the river-
side: ". . . the dragging wind and majesty of the cloud
full of splendor, and in it, swirled round by fire, a dark-
yellow moving object, a flying vehicle, flat, with rounded
edges, and surmounted by a glass bell of a bluish color.
When it landed, there descended from it archangels,
amidst wheels, flaring flames, and the pealing of trumpets." Along with the excited José Kakende came Hilário
Cordeiro to take the youth home with him again, as
tenderly as if he were his real father.

At the door of the church was a blind beggar, Nicolau.
When the youth caught sight of him he gazed at him
deeply and with his whole attention (they say his eyes
were the color of a rose!) and then he walked straight up
to the beggar and hastily handed him a bit of something
out of his pocket. No Christian soul could see that blind
man, sweating in the sun, without noting the irony of his
having to bear the heat of that burning orb and at the
same time be denied the ability to rejoice in the beauty
of the sun or the moon. The blind man fingered the gift
in his hand and then, instead of wondering what out-
landish manner of money it could be and then realizing it
was no money at all, brought it up to his mouth at once,
only to have the child who was his guide warn him that it
was not something to eat but only a seed from some kind
of tree pod. The blind man angrily put the seed away and
only planted it months later, long after the events soon
to be related had already taken place. From the seed

sprouted a rare and unexpected bluish flower, several contraposed flowers in one, all commingled impossibly in lovely confusion. The tints were of a kind not seen in our times; no two people could even agree on precisely what the colors were. But soon it wilted and withered away, producing no seeds nor shoots; even the insects had not had the time to learn to seek it out.

Just after the scene with the blind man, though, Duarte Dias appeared in the churchyard with some of his friends and servants, ready to make trouble and astonishing everyone by demanding that the youth go with him, on the grounds that because of the whiteness of his skin and his aristocratic ways, he must be one of the Resendes, Duarte Dias's rich relatives who had been lost in the earthquake; and that therefore, unless some definite news was received that the youth was no Resende, it was his responsibility to hold him in his custody. This proposal was promptly contested by Hilário Cordeiro, and the argument might easily have become a real altercation because of Dias's loud insistence, if he had not finally given in to the persuasion of Quincas Mendanha, a political notable from the capital, who was also purveyor for the Brotherhood.

Soon it became clear that Hilário Cordeiro was righter than he knew when he protected the youth so zealously. He began to be lucky in everything: all in his household were healthy and lived in harmony, and his business prospered. It was not that the youth gave him much overt help; he could hardly have been expected to do rough farm labor with his dainty, uncallused hands, as white and smooth as a courtier's. In fact, he spent most of his time dreamily wandering about here and there at will, exercising an airy freedom and a taste for solitude. People said he must be under some magic spell. Magic and delicate hands to the contrary notwithstanding, the youth did take an extremely important part in everything to do with the machinery and the tools used on the place. He was extraordinarily good at mechanics, inventing and repairing in the cleverest, most careful way. At those times he was wide-awake enough. He was also an astronomer, but one with the odd habit of continually watching the sky by day as well as by night. Another amusement of his was to light fires, and everyone noticed how eagerly he took part in lighting the traditional bonfires on St. John's Eve.

It was on that very St. John's Eve that the incident with the girl Viviana occurred, a story which has never been told accurately before. What happened was that when the youth, accompanied by the Negro José Kakende, came up and saw that the girl, though so pretty, was not amusing herself like the others, he went up close to her and gently, but startlingly, laid the palm of his hand delicately on her breast. And since Viviana was the loveliest of all the girls, the wonder was that the beauty of his deed in no way altered his vague melancholy. But her father, Duarte Dias, who had been watching, bawled out, over and over: "They've got to be married! Now they have to get married!" He declared that since the stranger, who was unmarried, had shamed his daughter, he would have to take her to wife, willy-nilly. Though the young man listened pleasantly to all this and made no objection, Duarte Dias never stopped bellowing until Father Bayão and some of the older men remonstrated with him for his nonsensical anger. Young Viviana soothed him, too, by her radiant smiles; from the moment of the youth's touch there was awakened in her an unending joy, a pure gift which she enjoyed for the rest of her life. Incomprehensibly, Duarte Dias later added to the general amazement, as we shall see.

He came to Casco Ranch on August 5, the day of the mass of Our Lady of the Snows and Eve of the Transfiguration, and asked to speak to Hilário Cordeiro. The youth was present, too, so otherworldly and graceful that he made one think of moonlight. And Duarte Dias begged them to let him take the young man home with him, not out of ambition or because he wanted to pretend to a rank he didn't have, nor out of any petty self-interest, but because he really wanted and needed to have with him one for whom his contrition and remorse had led him to conceive the strongest esteem and affection. He was so moved that he could scarcely speak, and copious tears flowed from his eyes. Those who heard him could not understand such a change in a man who had never been able to express any emotion at all except in some violent, impetuous way. However, the youth, bright as the eye of the sun, simply took him by the hand and, accompanied by the Negro José Kakende, led him off through the fields to a place on Duarte's land where there was an abandoned brick kiln. There he made signs for the men to dig, and they found a diamond deposit—or maybe a big pot of gold, as another story has it. Naturally, Duarte Dias thought he would become a very rich man after this, and he changed from that day on into a good, upright man, so his awestruck contemporaries claimed.

But on the Venerable St. Bridget's Day something more was heard of the imperturbable youth. It was said that the night before he had made one of his customary disappearances, but this time by way of the sky, at a time of dry thunder. All José Kakende would say was that he had secretly helped light nine bonfires in a pattern. Aside from that, he only repeated his old wild descriptions of a cloud, flames, noises, round things, wheels, a contraption of some sort, and archangels. With the first sunlight, the youth had gone off on wings.

Each one, in his own way, mourned his life long whenever he thought of the youth. They doubted the air they breathed, the mountains, the very solidity of the earth—but remembered him. Duarte Dias actually died of sorrow, though his daughter, the maiden Viviana, never lost her joy. José Kakende had long talks with the blind man. Hilário Cordeiro, like many others, said he felt he was half in his grave whenever he thought of the youth. His gleam remained when he was gone. That's all there is to tell.

• THE HORSE THAT

DRANK BEER

THE MAN'S COUNTRY HOUSE was darkened and half-hidden by the trees; you never saw so many trees around a house. He was a foreigner. My mother told me how he came the year of the Spanish flu, cautious and scared-like, to buy that place that was so easy to defend. From any of the windows of the house you could keep watch for a long distance, with your hand on your shotgun. In those days, he still hadn't grown so fat it made you sick. They said he ate all kinds of dirt: snails, even frogs, with armfuls of lettuce soaked in a bucket of water. You see, he ate lunch and supper sitting outside on the stoop, the bucket with the lettuce in it on the ground between his thick legs. The meat he cooked, though; that was real beef off a cow. What he spent most of his money on was beer, but he didn't drink it in front of folks. I used to pass by and he'd ask me: "Irivalini, *bisogno* another bottle, it's for the horse." I don't like to ask questions, and I didn't think it was funny. Sometimes I didn't bring it; but sometimes I did, and then he'd pay me back and give me a tip. Everything about him made me mad. He couldn't even learn to say my name right. Insult or just disrespect, I'm not the kind to forgive any mother's son either way.

Mother and I and a few other people used to pass by his gate on the way to the plank bridge over the creek. "Let him be, poor thing, he suffered in the war," my mother would say. There were always a lot of dogs around him, big fellows, guarding the house. One of them he didn't like. You could see the beast was scared and unsociable—it was the one he treated the worst—but even so, it wouldn't budge from his side, and though he despised it, he was always calling the poor devil. Its name was Mussulino.

Well, I brooded over the grudge I had against him, a bull-necked, paunchy man like that, hoarse and snuffling all the time, so foreign it turned your stomach—was it fair for him to have all that money and position, to come and buy Christian land with no respect for people who were hard up, to order dozens of beers and not even pronounce the word right? Beer? The fact was, he did have some horses, four or maybe three, and they sure led an easy life. He never rode any of them, couldn't have mounted them anyway. Why, he could hardly even walk. The old billy goat! He never stopped puffing on his little smelly cigar, all chewed up and drooled on. He had a good beating coming to him. So damned careful with his house locked up, like he thought everybody else was a thief.

He did admire my mother and treated her nice and

kind. With me, though, it was no use—I couldn't help hating him, even when Mother was so sick and he offered money to pay for the medicine. I took it; who can live off noes? But I didn't thank him. He probably felt guilty for being a rich foreigner. And it didn't do any good anyway; my mother, a real saint, went off into the dark, and damned if he didn't want to pay for the funeral. Later on he asked me if I'd like to come and work for him. I turned it over in my mind and argued with myself about what his reasons might be. He knew I was brave, that I had my pride, and that I could face up to anything; not many people in those parts were willing to look me straight in the eye. I thought it must be because he wanted my protection, day and night, against undesirable strangers and such. It must have been that, because he gave me hardly anything to do; I could fool around all I wanted to, so long as I had a weapon close by. But I did go to the store for him. "Beer, Irivalini. For the horse," was what he'd say, with a long face, in that language you could beat eggs with. I wished he'd cuss me! Then he'd see what was what.

The thing I couldn't get used to was all that covering up. That big old house was kept locked night and day; no one ever went inside—not even to eat, not even to cook. Everything went on out of doors. I reckon he hardly ever went in there himself, except to sleep or put away the beer—haw, haw—the beer for the horse. And I said to myself: "You wait, you pig, and see if one of these days I don't get in there, no matter what!" Maybe that was when I should have talked to the right people, told them what crazy things were going on, asked them to do something about it, put a bug in their ear. But it was easier not to.

Words don't come easy to me. And then, just about that time, they came—the strangers.

Two jokers from the capital. It was Seo Priscílio, the deputy police commissioner, who called me over to them. He said: "Reivalino Simple, these men you see here are officials; they're on the up and up." And then the strangers took me aside and tried to pump me. They wanted to know all about the man's habits, and they asked me all sorts of silly questions. I put up with it, but I didn't give anything away. What am I, anyway, a coati for dogs to bark at? I had my doubts too when I looked at the ugly mugs of those bundled-up rascals. But they paid me; a fair sum of money, too. The leader of the two, rubbing his chin with his hand, gave me a job to do: to find out whether my boss, "a very dangerous man," really lived by himself. And I was to take a good look, the first chance I got, and see if he didn't have, low down on his leg, the old mark of a collar, an iron ring, the kind criminals wear. And me, I piped up and promised to do it.

Dangerous, to me? Ha, ha. Maybe he had been a real man when he was young. But now he was paunchy, a high liver, lazy as they come, and all he wanted was beer —for the horse. The rat. Not that I had any complaints; I never liked beer much. If I had, I would have bought some for myself, or drunk his, or asked him for some; he would have given it to me. He said he didn't like it, either. And come to think of it, I guess he didn't. All he ever ate was that pile of lettuce with meat, his mouth so full it'd make you sick, along with a lot of olive oil, and he'd lick the drippings. He'd been kind of angry and suspicious lately; did he know about the strangers' visit? I didn't see any slave brand on his leg; didn't even try to look. Am

I some kind of errand boy to a chief deputy, one of those heavy thinkers who's always signing papers? But I did want to have a peek at that locked-up house, even if it had to be through a crack. And now that the dogs were tame and friendly, it seemed as if I could manage it. But Seo Giovânio got the idea that I was up to something, because one day he gave me a surprise: he called me over and opened the door. It stank inside, the way things do when the top's never taken off; the air didn't smell right. The parlor was big and empty; no furniture, just space. He let me look all I wanted to, on purpose it seemed, walked with me through several rooms, till I was satisfied. Ah, but later on I talked it over with myself, and I had an idea: what about the bedrooms? There were a lot of them left over; I hadn't gone into all of them by a long shot. Behind one of those doors I could feel something breathing—or did I only think that later? Oh, so the wop wanted to cheat me. Didn't he know I was smarter than he was?

Well, after a few days had gone by, very late on two or three different nights you could hear galloping out on the empty plain, like a horseman riding out at the pasture gate. Was the fellow fooling me, turning himself into a ghost or a werewolf? On the other hand, there was that trick his mind had of wandering off the track in a way I could never quite understand; that might explain part of it. What if he really kept some funny kind of horse always hidden there inside, in the dark house?

Seo Priscílio called on me one more time that week. The strangers were there with him on the quiet. I came in in the middle of the conversation: I made out that one of those two worked for the "Consulate." But I told them

everything, or a lot anyway, to get even. Then the strangers got Seo Priscílio all fired up to carry out their plan.
They wanted to stay under cover and let him go alone.
And they gave me some more money.

I hung around pretending to be deaf and dumb, just
twiddling my thumbs. Seo Priscílio came and spoke to
Seo Giovânio: what were those tales he had been hearing
about a horse that drank beer? He kept on pressing him,
trying to learn something. Seo Giovânio looked awfully
tired. He shook his head slow and weary and snuffled the
snot from his nose to the stump of his cigar; but he didn't
get mad at him. He kept putting his hand to his forehead:
"You wanta see?" Then he went off and came back with
a basket with lots of full bottles and a pail and poured it
all in, with the beer foaming up. He told me to go get the
horse: the light cinnamon-colored sorrel with the pretty
face. The animal trotted up raring to go—would you believe it?—with his ears twitching and his nostrils flared
and his tongue hanging out, and smackingly drank down
the beer. He enjoyed it clear down to the bottom of the
pail. You could see he was used to drinking all he wanted!
When had he been taught that trick, of all things? Well,
that horse just couldn't drink enough. Seo Priscílio looked
ashamed of himself, thanked Seo Giovânio, and went
away. My boss let out a whistle and looked at me: "Irivalini, times are getting bad. Don't leave the guns!" I approved of that even if I did have to laugh at his crazy ideas
and his tall tales. I still halfway hated him.

So when the strangers came back again, I told them
what I thought: that there must be something else in the
bedrooms in that house. This time Seo Priscílio came with
a soldier; he simply announced that he intended to search

all the rooms in the name of the law! Seo Giovânio, standing still and peaceful-like, just lit another cigar; he was
always cool and sensible. He opened up the house so that
Seo Priscílio could go in, and the soldier, too, and me. The
bedrooms? He went straight to one that was all bolted
tight. And lo and behold! There inside, big as a house, was
the queerest thing—was I dreaming?—a big white horse,
a stuffed horse. It was so exactly right with its square
face, like a hobby-horse; shiny-bright, white, clean, with
a long mane and fat hindquarters, tall as the one in the
church—a St. George horse. How could they have brought
it, or had it brought, and got it in there all put together?
Seo Priscílio's face fell; he couldn't get over it. He felt the
horse all over, but it wasn't hollow; it just had straw inside. Seo Giovânio, as soon as he was alone with me,
chewed on his cigar: "Irivalini, it's a shame the two of
us don't like beer, eh?" It sure was. I felt like telling him
what was behind all the goings-on.

But if Seo Priscílio and the two strangers weren't
suspicious any more, what about the other bedrooms in
the house, and behind the doors? They should have
searched all over and been done with it. Not that I was
going to remind them, not being the kind to pop my hand
up to be called on all the time. Seo Giovânio started talking to me again, after he had mulled things over a while:
"Irivalini, *ecco*, life is hard and men are prisoners . . ."
I didn't want to ask him about the white horse. Fiddle-
sticks. What did I care about it? It must have been his
horse during the war; it was probably his pet. "But
Irivalini, we love life too much." He wanted me to eat
with him, but his nose was dripping with snot and dribble,
and he sniffled and didn't bother to wipe it off, and every

inch of him stank of cigar smoke. It was awful to watch that man not feeling sorry for himself. So I went and talked to Seo Priscílio: said I wouldn't have anything more to do with those strangers who wanted to stir up trouble. I wouldn't play their two-faced game! If they came back I'd run them off the place, I'd cut loose, I'd fight them— just hold your horses! This is Brazil, and they were just as much foreigners as the boss was. I'm quick to draw a knife or a gun. Seo Priscílio knew it. But I don't think he knew about the surprise that was coming.

It happened all of a sudden. Seo Giovânio threw the house wide open. Then he called me: in the parlor, in the middle of the floor, was a man's corpse lying under a sheet. "Josepe, my brother," he said to me, looking all cut up. He wanted the priest, wanted the church bell to toll three times three, wanted the sad part to be just right. No one had ever known that brother of his who had run away from people and kept himself hidden. It was a respectable funeral. Seo Giovânio needn't feel ashamed before folks. Except that Seo Priscílio came beforehand—I reckon the strangers had promised him some money— and made us lift up the sheet for him to have a look. But all you could see was how holy-terrified we all were, and our staring eyes: the dead man had no face, you might say—only a great big gaping hole, with old healed-over scars, awful, no nose, no cheeks—you could see the white bones where his throat began, his gullet and his tonsils. "That's-a the war," explained Seo Giovânio, forgetting to close his silly mouth that was hanging open, all nasty sweetness.

Now I wanted to get out of there and go on my way; it was no good for me to stay there any longer in that crazy, unlucky place, with the trees so dark all around. Seo Giovânio was sitting outside, the way he had done for so many years. He looked sicker and older all of a sudden, with that sharp pain sticking into him. But he was eating his meat and the heads of lettuce from the bucket, and snuffling. "Irivalini . . . this life is . . . *bisogno. Capisce?*" he asked in his singsong voice, looking at me, his face purple. "*Capisco,*" I answered. I didn't give him an *abraço;* not that I was disgusted, just ashamed. I didn't want to cry, too. And then if he didn't do the damnedest thing: he opened the beer and watched it foaming out on the ground. "*Andiamo,* Irivalini, *contadino, bambino?*" he proposed. I said yes. Glass after glass, by the twenties, the thirties, I drank it all down. He had calmed down some by then, and when I went away he asked me to take the horse—the sorrel that drank beer—and that hangdog thin dog, Mussulino.

I never saw my boss again. I knew when he died, because he left the farm to me in his will. I had tombstones made and masses said for him, and for his brother and my mother. I sold the place, but first I cut down all those trees and buried the stuff that had been in that room I told you about. I never went back there again. No, I can't forget that one day—how awful I felt. The two of us with all those many, many bottles. When it happened, I thought I saw someone else come up suddenly behind us: the white-faced sorrel, or St. George's big white horse, or the poor, miserable brother. I, Reivalino Simple, *capiscoed.* I drank up all the beer that was left, and now I pretend it was me that drank all the beer in that house. Just so nobody will make any more mistakes.

✦ NOTHINGNESS AND THE HUMAN CONDITION

ONCE THERE WAS a rancher we called Uncle Man'Antônio, whose character was even more impressive than his outward appearance; he might have been the old king in some fairy tale not yet written, or the younger prince. But no one in my family, nor anyone else from my part of the country, really knew him.

His ranch, whose main house was a good ten leagues from any of his neighbors', was completely surrounded by the mountains, and itself stood on a very high peak, where the thinly translucent air received the full rays of the sun. In that rarefied air the mornings came gliding in, one like another, and the purples and rosy tints of the sunset gave no hint of the vagaries of the world's weather. Uncle Man'Antônio had bought much more land than he had inherited, but he was so retiring, so laconic and taciturn in conversation, that he almost never referred to these great holdings by their name but only—and then rarely, indeed almost never—in this fashion: "Back home . . . I'm going home . . ."

The two-story house was set on firm foundations and was high-roofed, long, and full of galleries and rooms which were never used. It smelled of fruit and flowers, leather, wood, fresh cornmeal, and cow dung. The house faced north and was set between an orchard of lemon trees and the handsome corrals. On the front of the house was a wooden staircase, with its forty steps arranged in two tiers leading up to a spacious veranda, in one corner of which there still hung, creaking, the rope that had once summoned the slaves from the quarters.

Awaiting Uncle Man'Antônio was Aunt Liduina, his wife, full of deep and immemorial affection, forever and forever faithful. And beside her his daughters, naïve, serious, and solicitous, and overflowing with love for him. Long before he reached the first gate, he was greeted with murmurs of the customary "God be with you" from various hired hands, natives of the region, who lived on ranches along the way. Each time he came home he stooped slightly when he entered the lofty front door, as if it were some low, mean entrance to a house not fit to welcome or shelter him. He lived according to some design of his own, and so there was no one who actually knew him except from afar. Then suddenly, one day he would be ascending the mountain on his way back from one of his journeys, scaling the precipitous paths, skirting precipices and crevasses and deep, dark valleys at tremendous altitudes. From the veranda, if the day was clear, they could see him when he was still many leagues off, a dot in the diaphanous air, seen at certain turns in the road, coming closer, then retreating, seemingly in no logical order. Persevering ever, Uncle Man'Antônio slowly advanced on his tireless, gentle mule, dressed in rugged attire which served as a rough kind of riding habit, though it was only his ordinary mud-colored khaki work clothes, worn without boots, chaps, or spurs. Every little while, by looking very attentively, they could make out his familiar, absent-minded gestures: the one he made from time to time of very slowly pushing something away from him; or the way he smoothed the wrinkles out of his forehead with his fingers, meanwhile pondering over what he intended to say *no* to, ready for anything, but seeming at times to doze off. Did he no longer even look at that fearful landscape?

Yes, he saw both the high mountain passes and the hellish, unbelievably deep abysses. He gazed at them long, as though making them an offering, somehow, of the best of himself—the prime of his life—in a kind of hope or expiation, sacrifices, struggles. In return, might he not, someday, be allowed to meet the King of the Mountains or the King of the Valleys, grateful for the tribute he paid them? For every imaginable thing exists and may one day be met.

Who knows what kinds of ideas—useless, original, inevitable—he thought to himself, in secret, without even letting them come into his own full consciousness. That is how it is. Each of us lives only his future past. He never felt thirst, loneliness, heat, or cold, nor ever complained of ordinary discomforts. He just hunched over, his head nodding a little, his mouth tightly shut, his breathing slightly labored. His sight had begun to fail at that time, weakened from too much looking. With a love never known before, he gazed from afar at the peaks and valleys. Perhaps he felt the need, this man, to face boldly whatever might be there? And finally he would reach home, after those arduous hours and the difficult ascents.

Then his wife, Aunt Liduina, died, with no warning whatever, without so much as time to sigh out an "Ay!" or to begin an interrupted Hail Mary. Without a moment's hesitation, Uncle Man'Antônio ordered all the doors and windows of the great, long house to be thrown wide open. And while the orphaned daughters embraced each other and laid out the beloved corpse, he incongruously visited every room one after the other, from end to end of the house.

In each room he looked out the windows with an urgent, interested gaze, his eyes traveling across the landscape, one portion of it after the other, as he had done in the room before and in the one before that. On his round of the house he saw dimly, at least, where the valleys and mountaintops were and where the horizon was—absolutely everything. When he cast a second glance around, he glimpsed the landscape from behind: the shadows of the valleys and of the monstrous hills, fading away as if on wings. Would he find help there, now that he was so in need of it? Since he no longer had either past or future, he decided to remain where he was, firm as a rock, despite all contradiction or resistance. He may have murmured, deep within him, serious and weighty things, soundlessly and past understanding.

Finally he returned to the women, to his Liduina who was lying in state, motionless under a mountain of flowers, all in accordance with the custom of the times, as they had wanted her to be. Since they shared a common sorrow, the daughters, though full of suspense and vague conjectures, nevertheless put their hopes in him for help. But he withdrew behind his outer self into ambiguous places and moments, as if life could be hidden; as if he could not be recognized behind his features. And so he remade what was malleable in him; he was now a different, more decorous, dependable kind of person, thinner, with palely blue eyes in his ashen, dark-complexioned face.

Looking at him now, one could see how his daughters might suddenly attain some unknowable healing grace from those hollow eyes, by remote, indescribable reflexes or signs. Only the youngest daughter, Felícia, cried out, addressing her father: "Oh, Father, is life nothing but treacherous vicissitudes? Can no one ever enjoy a time of happiness, in real security?" And he answered, slowly and carefully in his soft voice: "Make believe, little daughter. Make believe. . . ." Though only half understanding him, they could hope for no more. On saying these words, which henceforward would be his own forevermore, Uncle Man'Antônio lowered his head and gave his wife a light kiss. Then he and his daughters wept, but they did so out of a kind of freedom, like a stronger and more intrepid hope.

During long years of loving they had seen Aunt Liduina smile through her pain—suffering tribulations and going on living, in the common way of mankind—and now she was painfully missing from their habitual circle of affection. Aunt Liduina was only faint music and a memory.

But Uncle Man'Antônio refused to mourn; he was reasonable without seemingly having to make a great effort;

he was untragic, used none of the widower's words. True, he was grayer than before and a little more stooped. For a little while that was all one could say about him. He never spoke of his grief, and those around him wrongly assumed that he was again nothing, once more as he had been, voiceless, bodiless. But on the contrary, Uncle Man'Antônio was thinking. "Make believe!" he commanded at every opportune moment, but gently, gently. And he initiated a perfectly believable, practicable project —one that was duly begun.

Like the eager supporters they were, his barefoot farmhands, gaily and with alacrity, if not entirely professionally, exercised their muscles at his behest. He taught them the strong attack by means well known to this engineer, maker, and man of many parts; he joined them in their work and cheered them on by his murmured "Make believe, fellows, make believe. . . ." There was a half-smile on his lips, but he was hard on himself—adamant, indeed. Day after day he rose early and pushed and pulled them on to an industrious, constantly renewed bustle of felling trees and cutting brush, in what amounted to a complete remaking of the landscape—a hard-won reformation. Surely those hard-working, wrinkled men, dull and gaunt as they were, must never have thought of it as a matter of master and servants, but loved and respected him as one of themselves. So they eagerly went at the whole encircling forest, which had been surveyed from peak to valley by means of formulas and mathematical curves.

But as happens wherever big plans involve a period of confusion and disorder, the gossipy men thought of it as noddle-headedness, folly, an almost wicked piece of nonsense. However, Uncle Man'Antônio, with his "If it is what it is, then it is," just turned down the brim of his straw hat, half-closed his eyes against the sun, perspired, and coughed from time to time. He was one who knew how to nod his head, yes and no. Though his secretiveness kept anyone from knowing what the end of this was to be, he was awake and eager, one could see. But after all, was he not a man like other men, with flesh as weak as theirs? There must have been some other reason for his never tiring on that job no matter how late the hours. Indefatigable, he worked on or accepted setbacks, his mind busy all the while with the all and the nothing.

Artfully he assumed a new smile, all ingenuousness; he neglected all the good things of former days. His unvoiced plan, finally, and at its appointed time, was completed. And in such a way that his daughters saw that all was finished; and they were very sad.

What incredible, fruitless notion had led him to tear to pieces the view of the rising mountains which, in those yesterdays, their mother had seen and loved? In all that hewing and close-cropping on every side, literally nothing had been left untouched—not even the very slabs of outcropping rocks and little bunches of thick undergrowth and scrub—all had been made dry and barren. Such a wasteland had it become that his favorite daughter, Francisquinha, questioned him sorrowfully. Hadn't he lost all feeling, grown callous, in sin against their common grief? Silently he heard her out, and then, looking at her quietly, answered a little distantly, as if his thoughts were elsewhere: "Not really, daughter . . . not really." As he did so, he gave her an equivocal little smile, and said not another word. Instead, he pointed out the new landscape:

there the fields unfolded into the distance—clear, free, extending in a wide panorama without shadows, open to the eye and foot—the wide prairie lovely and green, in its unbelievable greenness of quick springing grass. Ah! —whatever had been done, then, and by whom, it was now an incredible fantasy come true. For here and there, as though left to give shade in the heat of the day to the cattle chewing their cud, sacred, each standing quite alone, were great showy paradise-nut trees, wild pump-woods at the edges of gullies, and trees that in February and March, and again in June and July, would be leafless and all one blaze of flower, the pink floss-silk and the purplish ruby-red one, each one magnificent. And others, many others. And not one, anywhere, except those trees which Aunt Liduina had loved best when she was alive— the greatest source of her happiness!

The daughters opened their eyes wide in amazement. They said little except by the tears they shed. It had become evident now that Uncle Man'Antônio had been and was becoming a true man. Living—and this most importantly—clothed in mortality and knowing happiness.

The fact was that in these matters to which all his attention had been given so arbitrarily, he had unintentionally and without guessing it acted as a prophet. For just then the price of cattle suddenly went up considerably, and all the ranchers began to buy more head and to improve and extend their pasturage. And so, in a sly way, Uncle Man'Antônio had hit on exactly the right move, coming out ahead of everybody else without even trying. And why should he, unassuming as he was, scorn to do so? He began to cast a shrewd eye also on the green slopes

of natural grasslands with which almost the whole mountain was covered: high—not man-made.

There was nothing to lead one to believe that he was
not acting from the same hard-headed motives as the rest;
but he did so in his own peculiar way: one slide followed
another in the projector. Did he march forward out of
honest shrewdness, seeing what he wanted and acting
accordingly? On the anniversary of Aunt Liduina's death
a year later, he proposed that they give a party just as if
she were alive and present, in order to give the lie to Fate.

The daughters having agreed, it was done. They were
now grown, their education finished. Some young cousins
came, their fancies turning lightly. . . . Uncle Man'Antônio was well pleased when he met them and saw how
things were with them. And his three beautiful daughters,
each one peerless, became engaged and were married
very soon after. In no time they went away with Uncle
Man'Antônio's sons-in-law, each to a different faraway
place. From that day on, he remained on the ranch as before. That was where he stayed, in his old deserted house,
under the blue, pinnacled peaks and measureless cliffs,
which soared above sheer-walled precipices, caverns, and
steeply descending abysses—in that mansion, suspended
—in vulnerability.

In his yearning to experience some tender affection,
did he miss his three daughters, whom he had seen reborn
through love, discovering happiness and courage, as we
know happens, in just being, in living and growing? His
daughters were now indivisible parts of a song, a faint
music like Aunt Liduina's memory.

Lonely he was, but not sad. Uncle Man'Antônio honored all mute, moving matter without wanting to keep it; he paid it respect even when making his most characteristic gesture of releasing something he held in his hands. Was he amusing himself, perhaps, when with another gesture he fondled, redeemed, plain, homey things? Nevertheless, very often, when he was filled with the greatest sense of well-being, he would get up and, without reasoning it out exactly, engage in some rough, hard labor—rain, sun, engagement. Did it seem to him as if the world-within-world were commanding him, imploring him, needing some of his substance to kindle it to life? Or was he seeking his own true self, in the future, in the wings of the mountain? He made believe; and he put his trust in the stillness as in the whirlwind.

During all this time he showed no sign of aging, in either his unflagging love of life or his absolute indolence; his hair had not even turned white like the pale mimosa, as it later did.

He was so prosperous, with his fields covered with cattle, that he could afford to spend as much as he liked. But Uncle Man'Antônio wanted nothing, though he was surrounded by all too many human frailties and greeds. He had evidently learned the power of events and actions to speak in muffled tones and piercing ones; and this was what deterred him from all avarice, from wanting anything in great quantities. He—the mortal. Did he really never think of the past? He did, yes, but, doomed and limited in his vision as he was, he discovered much more cause for hope both in the world around him and within himself.

In a universal sense, he would be granted the highest justice; it had to be thus. The storage bin must be swept

bare if it is to hold the new harvest; the half asks to be
made whole, the vacuum begs to be filled to overflowing.
This is the conclusion Uncle Man'Antônio reached one
day: that so it would be, if only one had faith. And in
truth, that is what happened. But it was the culmination
of a very confused history. And here it is. Well, then—

Gradually, taking first one piece and then another,
Uncle Man'Antônio distributed all his land among his
barefoot retainers, the blacks, the whites, the mulattoes,
the high yellows, the moccasined rascals, the field hands,
the cowboys, the hired men—everyone who was close to
him and had obeyed him. All of this was done quietly,
under cover, like a trade in silences, so as not to rouse
everybody's greed by letting the news get around that such
great acts of prodigality were taking place, and in such
an appalling fashion.

He used the money he had made to pay for the land he
pretended to sell in the usual way, sending it with great
punctuality to his daughters and sons-in-law, along with
tongue-in-cheek messages to make them believe the pay-
ments were genuine. It was a lucky thing that the daughters and sons-in-law did not want to have anything more
to do with Crooked Peak, that difficult-to-reach ranch in
the clouds, except to have it cut up and sold, all at once
or bit by bit. To him, though, it was still the place of all
places—icy-cold and crystal-clear.

At any rate, Uncle Man'Antônio never gave a thought
to what he should think of what he'd done. Was it Christian compassion that made him give his lands away? Or
was it madness and worse than madness? The great
circle is the one which returns on itself. From now on he
would have nothing he'd have to take care of. Whose are

the perilous deeps of the world and the cloud-piercing peaks of the mountains, and from whence do they come? "Make believe, my people. Make believe. . . ." This was all he said to them, and even so, when he used these words he did not smile but kept his feelings hidden.

His many servants, those very ones who had received the benefit of his benevolence, understood him no more than anyone else. When they found that his gift was made in earnest, they laughed aloud in their jubilation, at the same time half-afraid; too timid to leap for joy, they crossed themselves.

During those years when he had ignored them, he had never really known the character of his many hired hands —only that they existed, served him, lived, as they always have and always will. Were they essential now to the carrying out of his plan? Those men of his, necessary characters in that never-to-be-deciphered text?

Uncle Man'Antônio left everything in writing, all in proper form and written in his own still-firm hand, put in the terms of an agreement, exactly as he willed it and set it down. And in explaining his motives and the logic behind them, he kept in mind what the ordinary person thinks of things and the usual kinds of argument to which he is given, so that he would destroy any possible doubts. As will be seen, he seemed in his carefully planned protection to anticipate, as if clairvoyant, every accusation that would be brought against his former servants and hired hands for what was to come to pass, on so grand a scale, on that much later crimson night. He was careful to protect them by means of a written statement, dated long before what was to come.

He kept nothing for himself except the enormous old

house, built high on its airy perch, and with so gracious and wide a view that from there the world seemed bigger, translucent, though there were deceptive depths in its hidden foundations. Nothing. Perhaps, nothingness. He pretended he, too, had nothing; he himself made believe. As for the others, however much he might love them, he understood them not at all.

It became his habit to make believe that they were the owners, those others. They never understood him in the least. And they certainly did not love him, since they always had to fear his hidden self and respect his position, there in his palatial court, in all its majesty. Why didn't he just go away, once and for all, and be done with it, the dotty old scarecrow, that bats-in-the-belfry old bogey man? Sage, sedentary, out of his desire that they get ahead and never lose ground, he watched over them and kindly attended to their affairs, as their manager, overseer, and landlord. They still served him, just as they always had. But beyond all doubt they hated him with an immemorial savage hatred.

Uncle Man'Antônio, moving toward the all, the secret password, was withdrawing—from himself toward himself within himself. He no longer questioned anything— horizon or eternity—peak or zenith. And so he lived, carrying the burden of years, erect, serene, and doing a doing-nothing with all his might, in acceptance of the emptiness, the ever-repeated inconsequence, of his life; and he thought what he thought. Whether never, and when.

And while all this was going on, it happened. It happened—that hesitant step which no thought can follow. He died, like a thread passing through the eye of a needle.

He died; he made believe. They found him in a hammock, there in the smallest bedroom, no friend or lover near him —a passerby, a prince and alone, an inhabitant of this world.

And ah me, the shock made them dizzy and struck them dumb, filling them all with fear at the thought that such a man, a veritable seraph, could come so shelterless to his end; and from that sacred terror and almost unconscious hatred came the dread that death would bring on them a train of terrible evils and that outrageous vengeful punishments would be unleashed, to fall on them and their children from on high.

Nevertheless, since he was dead, they must pay the usual honor and respect to his body, human and hereditary, but unmaimed. They lit the four tall candles at his head and feet and laid him out, dressed in the stiff plum-colored serge and black boots they found, lengthwise on the table in the parlor, the largest room in the House. And there he rested at peace. And then they had to send notes and messages so that all the other people could come, the relatives and everyone who was not there but might possibly come from near and far. Tears were shed on the veranda. The bell was tolled.

The duties were all fulfilled, when, just at sunset, the House suddenly caught fire and was razed to the ground. Someone should certainly have been inside it at that hour, but not a soul was there.

And so the red bonfire, of unbelievable size, began to burn, as it would for days, rising higher and higher, visibly swallowing up as it crackled obstacle after obstacle, one thing after another, to feed its flames. It blazed up at each gust of wind, throwing high in the quivering air the particles of dung from the corrals, which were also burning, as was the tiered staircase with its forty steps, and the searing garden of lemon trees. Borne by the wind, fire, sparks, and debris were scattered for a league around, over the steep slopes, the gorges and caverns, as if, in a resplendence of fantastic winged billows, the whole mountain were on fire. A brilliance, a white incongruous clarity, a macabre radiance, transfixed the night.

In a ring facing the fire at a distance, women knelt and men leaped as they shouted, enfrenzied souls turned into demons in flame-filled air. They threw themselves on their faces in the dust, imploring that they be given something or nothingness, desperate to be at peace.

And when the dead body had been consumed, in his ashes he, the lord, began his journey through the earth, sepulchral sphere, and nothing more; and all this as the sum total of a thousand acts, each a result and a cause.

He—became the Predestined One—Man'Antônio, my Uncle.

❖ **THE MIRROR**

IF YOU WILL bear with me I will relate to you, not an adventure but an experiment into which I was drawn by an alternating series of reasoned arguments and intuitive perceptions. The cost in time, discouragement, and exertion was considerable, and I take credit for it, but without boasting. It surprises me, however, that I should have taken a different tack from everyone else and penetrated into a realm of knowledge that is still unfamiliar to others. You, for example, are a student and a scholar, yet I presume you have no idea of the real nature of—a mirror. Oh, of course you know something about physics and are familiar with the laws of optics. I refer to its *transcendent nature*. But then, everything that exists is the iceberg's tip of some mystery or other. Including facts. Or the lack of them. When nothing is happening, there is a miracle occurring which we do not happen to be able to see.

Let us get down to specifics. Your features are imprisoned by many mirrors; they all reflect your face, and you think you have your own appearance, a practically unchanging one, of which they give back to you a faithful image. But—which mirror? There are "good" and "bad" mirrors, those that flatter us and those that exaggerate our bad points; and there are those that are simply honest, of course. But at what point do you fix the level of that honesty or faithfulness? What do you, and I, and our fellow men really look like? If you say that photographs can tell us, I retort that not only do the same objections apply to the camera lens as to mirrors, but also the resulting pictures support rather than give the lie to my contention, inasmuch as they reveal signs of mystery superimposed upon the optical data, iconograph upon photograph. Even when pictures are taken immediately one after another, each will always be *very* unlike the others. If you have never noticed this, it is because we live out our lives incorrigibly unaware of the things that are most important. And what about masks, molded onto the face itself? They roughly approximate to the features, but they cannot reproduce the swift-changing expressions of the face or its dynamic movements. Don't forget that we are dealing with very subtle phenomena.

There remains the argument that anyone can look simultaneously at another person's face and at that person's reflection in the glass. Without resorting to sophisms, I refute the assumption. Such an experiment, which, incidentally, has never been *rigorously* carried out, would lack any scientific value in view of the inevitable distortions of a psychological kind. If you make the attempt, you can expect some remarkable surprises. And besides, a simultaneous view is impossible if one takes into account the flow of instantaneous changes. Yes, time is a treacherous sorcerer. . . . And our own eyes, no matter how keen they may be, are marred by fundamental distortions, defects we grew up with and which have become more and more a part of us. Infants see objects upside-down at first, which explains their awkward fumbling; only little by little are they able to correct their precarious view of the position of external objects.

Other flaws, however, and more serious ones, remain. Our eyes are the portal of error; doubt your own eyes, not me. Ah, my friend, while the human species struggles to impose some measure of routine and logic on the throbbing world, something or someone opens chinks and crevices in it at every turn in order to mock us. . . . And what happens then?

Mind you, my objections have been limited thus far to the flat mirrors in everyday use. What about the others—concave, convex, parabolic—not to mention the possibility of still others, as yet undiscovered? A tetra-, or four-dimensional, mirror, for example? Such a hypothesis seems to me by no means absurd. Mathematical specialists, once they have acquired the necessary mental dexterity, have succeeded in building four-dimensional objects, using small, varicolored cubes like those children play with. Can you doubt the other, then?

I see that your initial distrust of my soundness of mind is beginning to wear off. But let us not stray from the pedestrian, the commonplace. We laugh at those distorting mirrors in funhouses which turn us into attenuated or ballooning monstrosities. But we owe our exclusive use of flat looking glasses (after all, the curves of a teapot make a passable convex mirror and a polished spoon, a reasonably good concave one) to the circumstance that humankind first looked at itself in the surfaces of quiet waters: lakes, marshes, and fountains, learning by imitating them to fashion those metal or glass utensils to which I have alluded. Still, Tiresias did warn the beautiful Narcissus that he would live only as long as he never saw his own face. . . . Yes, we have reason to be afraid of mirrors.

For my part, I have been afraid of them ever since childhood, out of an instinctive suspicion. Animals refuse to look into them, too, aside from a few credible exceptions. I am from the outback, just as you are; and where we come from they say that when you are alone you should never look into a mirror during the small hours of the night, for sometimes, instead of your own reflection, some other, frightful visage may appear there. I, however, am a materialist, a rational person who keeps his feet firmly on the ground. Satisfy myself with fantastic nonexplanations? Of course not. Then what frightful vision could it be? Who is the Monster?

Might my fear not be atavistic? Mirrors inspired superstitious fear in those primitive peoples who believed that a person's reflection was his soul. And, as a general rule, superstitions make a fertile starting point for scientific investigation. The soul of the mirror—what a splendid metaphor! Other peoples, incidentally, identified the soul with the body's shadow; and surely you have not overlooked the polarity: light-darkness. Was it not formerly the custom to cover the mirrors, or turn their faces to the wall, when someone in the house died? If, besides utilizing them in performing imitative or sympathetic magic, clairvoyants make use of mirrors in the form of crystal balls within which they dimly glimpse the future, is it not because time changes its speed and direction on the other side of the looking glass? But I am too prolix. As I was telling you . . .

It was in the lavatory of a public building, as it happens. I was young, complacent, and vain. Unthinkingly, I looked . . . But let me explain: there were two mirrors, one on the wall and the other on a side door, which were open at right angles. And what I glimpsed for a second was a human figure in profile which was antipathetic to the last degree, repulsive, utterly hideous. It nauseated me; it inspired me with hatred, fear, horror; it made my flesh creep. And it was—as I realized immediately—myself! Do you think I could ever forget such a revelation?

From that day on I began to search for myself—in the surface of mirrors, in their smooth, polished depths, in their cold flame. As far as I am aware, no one ever tried to do such a thing before. Whoever looks in the glass does so with an affectionate partiality, a more or less fallacious presupposition. No one really thinks of himself as ugly; at the most, we are dissatisfied with ourselves at certain times for temporarily falling short of a preformed aesthetic ideal. Do I make myself plain? What we are attempting to do is to verify, to adjust, working on the basis of a subjective, pre-existent ideal form; in other words, to enlarge the illusory image with successive new layers of illusion. I, on the other hand, was acting as an impartial investigator, absolutely neutral. I was hunting down my true form, driven by a disinterested, even im-

personal curiosity, not to say a scientific urge. It took
months.

They were certainly instructive ones. I employed all
sorts of ingenious tricks: the lightning-swift turn for a
second glance, the look askance, the long, oblique stare,
the counter-surprise, the feint with the eyelids, the am-
bush of the suddenly turned-on light, the incessantly
varied angles. Above all, I was inexhaustibly patient. I
regarded myself at certain designated moments—in
anger, fear, beaten or exacerbated pride, extreme joy or
sadness. But enigmas opened out before me. If you face
your reflection objectively when feeling hatred, for example, the hate ebbs and flows, enormously multiplied;
and you realize that, in effect, a man can hate only himself. Eyes eyeing eyes. I learned this: our eyes are eternal.
They alone remained still, immutable, in the center of
the mystery. At least, when they were not mocking at me
from behind a mask. The rest of my face changed continually. You, like other people, do not see that your face
is merely a perpetual, deceptive motion. You don't see
because you are inattentive, dulled by habit; still embry-
onic, I should say, not having developed the most necessary new perceptions. You don't see, just as we are not
ordinarily aware of the lateral and rotating movements
of this planet Earth, on which your feet and mine are
set. Blame me if you wish; I know you understand me,
nevertheless.

As it was, I had to penetrate the veil, see through that
mask, in order to expose the heart of the nebula—my true
countenance. There must be a way. I pondered, and was
rewarded by a positive inspiration.

I concluded that since the disguise of the *external face*

was composed of diverse mingled elements, my problem was to submit these to a visual blockade or perceptive annulment, blotting out each element one at a time, beginning with the most rudimentary, the grossest, the least meaningful. I took the animal element as a start.

That each of us resembles the *facies* of a specific animal is, of course, a fact. I am merely stating this truth; far be it from me to expound on such matters as metempsychosis or the theories of biogenetics. I learned something about it, as it happens, from a master in the science of Lavater. What do you think of these resemblances? Sheep heads and horse faces, for example: a glance at a crowd or a close look at your acquaintances and you see that there are a great many of those. But my inferior double in the scale of evolution was—the wildcat. I made sure of it. And so, after meticulously singling out these animal elements, I would have to learn *not to see* in the glass the features that resembled those of the great feline. I flung myself into the task.

Forgive me for not describing in detail the method or methods I used, alternating the most searching analysis with a strenuous power of synthesis. Even the preparatory stages would have been enough to discourage anyone less willing to undertake the arduous. Like every educated man, you are familiar with yoga and must have practiced at least its more elementary techniques. I even know of atheistical thinkers and philosophers who cultivate the "spiritual exercises" of the Jesuits in order to deepen their powers of concentration as well as their creative imagination. . . . I do not deny that I resorted to some very empirical methods: gradations of light, colored lamps, pomades that glowed in the dark. I refused only one ex-

pedient as vulgar if not deceitful: introducing other sub-
stances into the glass and silvering of the mirrors. But
it was principally in the method of focusing and at the
same time partially distracting my sight that I must needs
become skillful: I had to look without seeing. That is,
without seeing in "my" face what remained of the beast.
Did I succeed?

You must understand that I was pursuing an experimental reality, not an imaginary hypothesis. And I can
tell you that I was making real progress in the experiment. Little by little, the field of vision of the mirror
showed gaps in my face, with those excrescences attenuated, almost entirely blurred out. I persevered. At this
stage, though, I decided to deal simultaneously with the
other nonessential, illusory features. Thus, for instance,
the hereditary element—the likenesses to parents and
grandparents—which is also, in our faces, an evolutionary
residue. Ah, my friend, not even the chick in the egg can
be wholly solipsistic. And then I had to subtract the re-
sults of infectious passions, whether manifest or latent;
whatever was brought out by the disorder of transitory
psychological pressures. And along with every trace of
other people's ideas and suggestions, the ephemeral in-
terests with neither sequel nor precedent, connections nor
profundity. It would take days to explain it all. I would
rather that you took my statements at their face value.

As I grew more and more a master at excluding, ab-
stracting, and extracting, my visual schema was cloven
by serious cracks like a cauliflower or a shepherd's purse,
became a mosaic, and then frankly cavernous, like a
sponge. And it grew darker. At about that time, in spite of
the care I took of my health, I began to suffer from head-

aches. Was it because I was turning into a veritable coward? Forgive me for the embarrassing change of key with which I am forced to make such a human confession, to introduce this note of inexplicable and unworthy weakness. Remember Terence, though. Ah, yes, the Ancients: it occurred to me that they represented Prudence as an allegorical divinity entwined in the coils of a serpent, and holding a mirror. I abandoned my experiment at once. And for months I refused to look at myself in any kind of mirror at all.

But once in the common daily round of coming and going, we are lulled into forgetting almost everything. Time, in a long enough span, is always serene. And it may be, too, that I was spurred on by a subconscious curiosity. One day . . . Forgive me; I am not seeking a novelist's effects by purposely keying up every situation to a higher pitch. I will simply say that I looked into a mirror and was not there. I saw nothing. Only the smooth surface, empty, scattering light like the open sun or purest water, covertly all. Had I no features, no face at all? I touched myself repeatedly. But there was only the unseen. The fictive, without visible evidence. What was I—the transparent gazer? I turned away abruptly, so agitated that I could scarcely stand and almost fell into an armchair.

The faculty I sought had been working in me quite by itself during those months when I rested from my labors. I turned to face myself again. Nothing. I was appalled: I could not see my eyes. In the bright burnished nothing, not even the eternal was reflected!

My progress toward a gradually simplified face had ended in its reduction to complete facelessness. The conclusion was a terrible one: had I no inner, personal,

autonomous existence? Could it be that I . . . had no
soul? That what I had supposed to be my *self* was no
more than animal survival, a few inherited features, unbridled instincts, strange passionate energy, a tangled
network of influences, all fading into evanescence? The
mirror's luminous rays and empty face told me exactly
that—with strict infidelity. And was it the same with
everyone? We were little more than children, then—
the *élan vital* was nothing but spasmodic impulses, bolts
of lightning among the mirages of hope and memory.

But you are no doubt thinking that my mind has wandered off the track, confusing the physical, the hyper-
physical, and the metaphysical, without the slightest hint
of balanced reasoning or any logical marshaling of facts
—I realize that now. You must be thinking that nothing
I have said is consistent, that none of it proves anything.
Even if every word of it were true, it would still be
nothing but a vulgar, self-induced obsession, the absurd
conceit of expecting the psyche, the soul, to be reflected
in a mirror. . . .

I admit that you are right. The fact is, however, that I
am a very poor storyteller and have put the inferences
before the facts: the ox behind the cart and the horns
after the ox. Forgive me. And let the chapter's end throw
light on what has so far been recounted awkwardly and
with too great precipitancy.

These are occurrences of a very intimate kind and a
most peculiar character. I relate them to you under your
pledge of secrecy. Because I am ashamed, I cannot re-
count everything in detail. I abridge them.

It was only later, years later, after I had gone through
a period of great suffering, that I confronted myself again

—but not quite face to face. The mirror showed myself to me. Listen, and I will try to tell you. For some time I could see nothing. Then, finally, after some time had passed—the faint beginnings of a sort of cloudy light, which little by little essayed a feeble sparkle and radiance. Its slightest ripple stirred my emotions. Or perhaps it was already part of my emotion. What faint light was that emitted by my face, only to be stopped just beyond it, reflected, surprised? Draw the appropriate inference for yourself, if you will.

These are things that we should never observe; not, at least, beyond a certain point. Things I discovered much later—my final discovery I made in a mirror. By then, if you will forgive this detail, I felt love—that is, I had learned resignation and so happiness. And . . . yes, I saw myself again, my face, a face; not this one which your reason attributes to me, but a not-quite-face— scarcely outlined—barely emerging, like a pelagic flower born of the abyss. . . . It was no more than a child's small face, even less than a child's. And nothing more. Will you never understand?

Should I tell you, or should I not, what I perceive, discover, deduce? Is it so? Am I groping for the obvious? I am searching backward. Can this disjointed world of ours be the plane—the intersection of planes—where the finishing touches are put to our souls?

If so, then "life" is a perilous, solemn experience, whose technique—part of it at least—demands a conscious jettisoning, a clearing away, of whatever obstructs the growth of the soul or buries it under rubble. Then comes the *salto mortale* . . . I use that expression not because it was Italian acrobats who revived the art of the somer-

sault, but because common phrases, dulled and deadened
by use, require a new touch and timbre. . . . And the
problem-judgment survives in the simple question: "Do
you exist yet?"

Yes? But doesn't that mean the irremediable destruction of our concept of life as an agreeably haphazard
business, without reason or purpose, a vale of absurdity?
I say no more, but I respectfully await your opinion on
these matters. I welcome any objections you may design
to express to me, your obedient servant, a newly made
friend, but nevertheless your companion as a lover of
science, with all its misguided successes and its halting
quantum jumps forward. Well, what is your considered
judgment?

❋ CAUSE AND

EFFECT

A COW WAS traveling on the road to Tabocas. She walked
down the middle of the road like a Christian, a little red
cow of a deep, solid, cinnamon color. She lifted her hindquarters a little in a gentle, rhythmic trot, her hooves
beating up dust from the ground. She never hesitated at
the crossroads. Shaking her horns, which were curved
like a crown, and lowering her head, she kept to the route
that would lead her straight to the river, and beyond the
river, at the edge of the day, to the lands of a certain
Major Quitério and the ranch of Pãodolhão.

At Arcanjo, where the road skirts the town, she was
noticed, and, seeing that she was a runaway, some men
tried to beat her back; she disengaged herself energetically and went on her way. On the edges of pastures the
ani birds, crossing her path in their flight, thought better

of their intention of perching on her back. She stopped to drink in Gonçalves's creek, which had dried up to a trickle of water. Tinamou hunters were shooting off their guns in the field. Barking from another direction made her take refuge in some fenced-in land that was overgrown with brush. Now some women gathering firewood were running away from her. She knew how to keep her distance from the riders she met, sticking close to the fence and looking innocent: lowering her head and craftily pretending to graze as long as she had to. A league farther on, though, on the Antonios' land, she broke into a slouching gallop as she passed some corrals where she heard people talking. That was not where she was headed. Old Uncle Terêncio, at the door of his house, remarked to his companion: "Whose cow's that, m'boy?" "She ain't ours, Daddy." She went her sure way; by love, not by chance.

The little cow had run away from Pedra ranch, very early in the morning—between the first song of the orioles and the third cock's crow—with the sun coming up in her face in a sky that was almost her color. She came from a herd of high-spirited cattle that had been transported by drovers. She had been driven from Pãodolhão, the place where she had been born and bred; and she was in the clutch of the homesickness that afflicts backlands cattle when they find themselves in unfamiliar territory, in October, just before the thunderstorms begin. And so the mouth of the road had swallowed her up—on her way to the where-to paths—facing the rising sun.

When he heard the news, Seo Rigério, owner of Pedra, said: "That she-devil." He was a high-up man to take notice of such a little thing. His informants told him her brand was that of a big rancher who lived a long way off.

His cowhands were posted and ready. This Seo Rigério had several sons on the place. He had no need of them; but only see how this story came to pass.

One of the boys, a fine young man, suddenly got a notion to take up the challenge. He tied his lasso onto the crupper and asked: "Is she a little cherry-red cow?" He mounted his horse; couldn't have said what had put him there or whether he could do it. He took the main road, riding with a light spur. Not knowing his way. Pointed from west to east.

Back to the cow. The head start she had didn't seem like enough to her. Coming up to a hill at a brisk walk, she did not even stop to eat grass in the ditches; she pulled off tufts of it as she went, still a prey to a dull, aching anxiety. When she was going uphill her head nodded as she toiled up disjointedly. Downhill, it was chasm-bordering, splay-legged, setting her course. Once on flat ground, she began to trot. Now she glimpsed other cows in an open field. She looked at them, craned her neck, and mooed—her mooing filled the whole melancholy countryside. It was a big blue-and-white day above dust and woodlands. The sun was full.

Now the young man was getting his bearings. He could see the horizon, and that was all he needed. He knew about runaway cows: how they have their own ways of blazing a trail so they can find their way home. In the meantime, he inquired of passersby for news of the fugitive. His chamois-colored horse bestirred himself and went into a new, swifter gait. The horse knew what sort of thing time was, and could appreciate an impromptu adventure. He jogged along, long, long, lending hooves to fancy. The land was parched. Rainless weather, red-earth plains, dusty, treeless tableland, featureless fields. The young man was getting weary, and he rested for a good long time. Afterward he was anxious to make up for lost time. He pressed on.

The little cow took advantage of her good head start. Here she was stopped by a high fence that kept on following her, right beside her, too close, too close. It led to a stream. The cow waded into it, making her way through the water. Three times smart. Until she was unluckily checked by another fence. She went back a way —broke into a run—and jumped over the fence in a sudden rush, with a leap that was almost flight. She was winning. And the red cow disappeared from view, bobbing in a dancing step, her tail swinging. The enemy was coming up behind her.

The young man, coming through the empty world, felt a calling as though he had been commanded to go where he was going. He felt irritation creeping up on him. He thought of thinking better of it and turning back, of leaving the whole business for another day. He thought of a word to call himself: imbecile. Discouraged, hardly going forward at all, he could always go back. Where was that animal taking him? But then, on the other hand, he had hardly started—it was just as easy to go forward as back —he didn't know what to do—well, he'd have to go on. If he went back without her he would be laughed at. Why had he come, anyway? The day was sad all around. Only a little flowering of leafless trees on the hills: the dark July purple of the jacarandas, the mimosa trees in their August yellow. All he could see were the far perspectives of a painting. The absurd air. Flat maps. The amazing sky. He examined the ground, looking for a trace. Now the great shadow of a cloud darkened the countryside. The youth gazed keenly into the distance. Suddenly he clapped his hand to his forehead and gave an exclamation. The curtain had been drawn back: there she was. The little cow, exhaling dust. Then and there he got his sights on her. The shape, looking about the size of a person, scaling the ridge of the hill. Well, if that didn't beat the devil! She seemed to shrink in size as she stood out, for a second, on the curved line of the ridge. Then she sank over the other side and was hidden from his view. She was surpassing her destiny.

All this time the young man was spurring his good horse and gaining on the cow. He kept a constant, sharp lookout; with his eyes he could follow the trail she was making. He was pursuing the landscape. A mottled vastness of gray and yellow was gathering itself; and yellow, too, was gathering in the sky. As the sun veered down the sky, expanses of the scorching plain were smoking: high, higher, blue, the smoke faded into the air. The youth—life unfolding before him—thought to himself: "Let what comes, come."

Then he was climbing the hill himself and could see even farther: the valleyed foothills before the doors of distance, and a river in its lowlands, slipping between its palmy banks. A smooth bright river, flowing with invisible movements. As though cutting the world in two, it crossed the road—without a sound. The shadows near its banks might have been black holes.

After her turns and detours, the little cow reached the last feathers of plume grass on the edge. With stolen rapidity, she was going to end her banishment. A little moving object—almost as if the two horns were swim-

ming by themselves—the red cow was crossing that river
in the late afternoon, in September. Under a sky open to
the night and calling to the smoke vapors.

And now the gold sketching of sunset. The youth and
his good mount, following the contours of the landscape.
On the way to the river he saw no birds, for they were already settling themselves in their nests. At the riverbank
at dusk, he thought how foolish it would be to run the
risk of calamity over nothing. He paused, considering
both sides. He could hear no vesper bell ringing. Would
he have to lose everything to win out? Since it was a case
of half one thing, half the other, he thought: nevermore,
evermore . . . Seo Rigério's son. Yes, he could cut short
the fatal pursuit and be quit of it. He hesitated, had it not
been for something, he did not know what—a sudden,
mystical yearning. He was at the crucial turning point of
the drama! He bent to unlace his boots. And waded in—
courage in his breast. Breasting the trans-wet-quil waters.
That was a river and a half. Now he was on the other side.

"The cow?"—he was shortening the distance between
them with a sharp spur and a loose rein. But the cow was
an artful one; she'd trick him if she could. In the meantime, night had overtaken them both. And his chamois-
gray horse was beginning to feel the effects of the long
lope under the saddle: his legs wobbled; he was drooping,
almost throwing his rider forward.

They went on in the blindness of night—to the home
of the mother of pitchnight: cow, man, cow—galloping
transients. "Up and down, where's Pãodolhão? Who's the
owner? Where's his home?" Fields were burning on distant slopes, clear to the top of the mountain: sparks—
the first stars. Hurrying on. The youth in his blind obses-

sion. He ached in every muscle, no longer able even to feel despair. The black shiver of the trees. The world between the stars and the crickets. Halflight: nothing but stars. Where, and whither? The cow was the one who knew: out of love for her own place.

She arrived, they were arriving, they were in the pastures of the vast fazenda. The cow loomed up in the night. She lowed wrenchingly. Lowed again. A berry of light, far off. Was it only a will-o'-the-wisp? Lights dotted the darkness: the windows of the big house. The house of a Major Quitério.

The youth and the cow came in through the main gate to the corrals. The young man dismounted and began to climb the steps under astonished eyes. He had so much to explain.

How well come he was!

To a circle of people. To the four young ladies of the house. To one of them, the second oldest. She was tall, fair, and amiable. She disconcealed herself from him. Had they unexpected each other? The youth understood himself. He saw what had happened in a different light. Of the cow, he would say to her: "She's yours." Was a transformation taking place in their souls? And all at the behest of life. There is nothing absurd: the honey of enchantment comes at this point in the tale, and the ring of the enchanted. They loved each other.

And the cow—hey diddle-diddle, the cow came home.

MY FRIEND
THE FATALIST

ONE DAY an insignificant little man, newly arrived in town, came to My Friend's house to ask his advice on a matter of life and death, My Friend being a man of vast knowledge and understanding, a poet, professor, ex-cavalry sergeant and lieutenant of police. Perhaps because of his breadth of experience, he often declared: "In society no man can be truly human. What humanity we see must be considered a kind of miracle, since there is no rational explanation for it." My Friend was a fatalist.

That day at that precise time, we were out in his back yard at target practice, using rifles and revolvers in turn. My Friend has the calm assurance that no one in the world ever knew how to shoot as well as he—was as accurate a shot or as quick on the trigger; he used up several boxes of bullets a day. He was speculating in a desultory way: "No one ever understood the way things really are except the Greeks. Nothing happens by chance." Fatalistic as a china plate in a shooting gallery, My Friend was. Just then someone came to tell him that the little man was asking for him.

You could see by his dress and the way he carried himself that he was from out back. He looked as if he were in his late twenties or even thirties; he must have been a good deal younger, though. Just dried up and wrung out. Stiff as a statue, poor fellow, with a solemn, weathered face; his back bent by hard work, his hands horny from hoeing. My Friend, after telling him to have a seat and wait a moment, continued our conversation in a low voice. I think he wanted a chance to study the man by glancing at him out of the corner of his eye every little while before making a final judgment. He said: "One's fate is a matter of links in a connected series, cause chained to effect—independent of birth, time and place . . . or karma . . ." The fact is that My Friend was a man, make no mistake about that; he was no character in a fable, I'll have you understand. The visitor was sitting on the edge of his chair, feet and knees together, holding his hat with both hands; all of him decently clean and poor.

Asked his name, he said it was José So-and-So but called, by your leave, Zé Halfback. You could tell that he was a very disciplined kind of man; he was not even especially nervous. It was his sense of the gravity of the occasion which tangled his speech: "I'm a man of the law. . . . I have a cousin who's a court clerk—but he can't help me. . . . I am a strong believer in law and order. . . ." My Friend murmured something like: "We live not under the law, but by Grace." He was quoting from the Epistles of St. Paul, so I knew he hadn't cottoned to Zé Halfback. But the little man, though nailed to the cross, feeling himself belittled, almost dishonored—threatened, even—was bound and determined to say his piece no matter what. He picked up his hat, which had fallen to the ground, and dusted it with his hand.

Then he made the following statement: He told us he was married, by both civil and church rites; that he had no children; and that he had been living in a village called Priest's Father. He lived in such harmony with his wife that he was able to enjoy life's ordinary pleasures and found nothing disagreeable about his hard work. But, on an unlucky day, there had appeared a rowdy stranger who had turned his life into hell by shamelessly making up to his wife, ogling her lustfully. . . . "What's his name?" interrupted My Friend, who knew the life history of every outlaw in South Minas. "Herculinão, surname Socó," the man informed him. My Friend turned to me and growled: "A real hell-raiser." It was certainly true that this Herculinão Socó deserved not a particle of human sympathy, in contrast to young Joãozinho do Cabo-Verde, for example, who was notorious in two states, but who, when he became acquainted with My Friend—"a man of such illustrious integrity"—decided to cross over for good to the São Paulo side of the state line so as to keep out of trouble. Though he knew nothing about the affair, Zé Halfback nodded and went on with his story.

In order to nip an unpleasant situation in the bud, he had acted prudently; patience always pays. He had let himself be humiliated and had turned the other cheek. But the other man, despicable blackguard that he was, far from mending his ways, grew more and more shameless, more and more insolent. "He won't follow the rules. You can't reason with a man with an evil mind. And I'm not the man for . . ." If he wasn't willing to act, he'd just have to put up with his misfortune. He could not even complain to the authorities; there wasn't any law in Priest's Father. His wife could no longer so much as set foot outside her own door without the man's coming over to eat her up with his eyes and insult her with his propositions. "And things were getting worse and worse, all because of that hairy goat." Zé Halfback was leaning so far over toward us that he almost fell off his chair. My Friend encouraged him with a "What gall!" whereupon he set his hat in his lap and sat up straight again.

One fright, one vexation followed another, and it got to the point where there was no help for it: he and his wife made the decision to move on. "It was a hard break to make, being as we were so poor. Besides, we knew we'd miss Priest's Father; we were very well thought of there. But if we were to respect God and obey the law, there was nothing else we could do. We set out for a village called Refuge. . . ." In Refuge they managed to acquire a cabin, a field, and an orchard. But before very long the same man he had mentioned before turned up, still up to no good, still full of his obsession, and settled there too. His obstinate persistence turned him into such a single-minded brute that soon everyone in town was afraid of him. Hating what they had to do, and at an even greater sacrifice, José Halfback and his wife made their secret escape from Refuge.

And all because of that beast. "By Jove!" ejaculated My Friend, going to make meticulous adjustments to a rifle that hung askew on the wall. The room looked like no other parlor anybody ever saw, it was so full of rifles, pistols, and shotguns. "This one has a very long range," he said, with a rather sinister laugh. He sat down again, though, and smiled pleasantly at José Halfback.

But a shadow had fallen over the little man's face.

Was he actually going to cry?

He went on: "We came here, with him right on our trail, disturbing the peace just the way he did before. He's like an octopus, he won't let me out of his hooks. Wherever I go, that fellow's right on my heels. . . . I have to watch my step so as not to lock horns with him." He hesitated a moment. Then he raised his voice for the first time. "I ask you, is that right? Hasn't he gone too far? Is he an outlaw? On the wanted list? He'll try any kind of skulduggery, that I know. Here in the city they say you can get justice. I'm only a poor man. But I want the law to punish . . ." Having said this much, he closed his mouth and pleaded silently, with eyes like a hound's.

My Friend did nothing but turn his face so that he was looking at the rifle. Perfectly serious, he let a long minute pass. That, and nothing more, not saying a word. He fixed his eyes squarely on the gun, at the same time taking rapid squints in the little man's direction out of the corner of his eye. He willed him to look at the rifle too, as if to drive the lesson home. But the little man still didn't understand that he was pointing at anything. "And so what am I to do?" he asked the direct question.

My Friend turned as deaf as a duck. He blew on his fingers. His eyes were glued to the gun on the wall, and at the same time he glanced sidelong at the other man. It was finally accomplished. The little man's eyes were opened—he woke up. At last he had understood the key to the puzzle. He said: "Oh-h-h." And laughed: at the causes and their effects. All at once he stood up; he could carry on now—by himself.

Perplexed no longer, he was on his way. He expressed his thanks; he was in high spirits again; his guardian saint was with him. He was on the point of leaving. My Friend said nothing but: "Would you like some coffee— or a little rum?" but the man replied, prudently: "Maybe I will have some . . . later." Nothing more was said, My Friend shook his hand. Yes, off went José Halfback.

Was My Friend, that intrepid man, going to let him cope all by himself? His comment was: "Barrel or butt." The little man was so vulnerable, such a lightweight, so weak. Was he the man for a struggle between titans? My Friend, on the other hand, was master of chaos; and now he was examining his weapon to see that the cylinder was full. Then he said: "Let's follow our Achilles, who is in need of aid." And thus it was.

We followed him.

He was walking along quite fast.

We had to quicken our pace.

And then—with no warning—the chain of events began to spin out. There, brought by fate, was Herculinão, that other man, the man who did not obey the rules. My Friend let out a canine sort of half-sneeze, as was his wont whenever he smelled gunpowder.

And . . . it was: fire, with the swiftness of an angel; and Herculinão, dead, fell crash! to the ground, square-dab in the middle of the street. There's nothing quite like the path of a bullet, and—how beautiful and how brief is life!

But how was it that only two shots were heard, though

three guns had been drawn? Herculinão had had no time
to fire. What with another bullet in his heart. A slow man.

Halfback ejaculated: "That Judas . . ."

No such excitement on the part of My Friend. He spoke
a polysyllabic "Ah-h-h," but without wasting any emotion
on it. He said: "Isn't it true that everything is written and
foreordained? Today this man met his fate. The Greeks
. . ." Then: "But Necessity has hands of bronze . . ."
and then: "He was resisting arrest, and we can prove it."
Thus, he metaphysicked a "Nay" to Fate.

Without bell-ringing and alarms, he saw to it that
Herculinão was speedily removed to the grave that had
been dug to his measure.

Then he invited us to lunch, and Zé Halfback was the
guest of honor.

My Friend was meditative. He said: "This Earth of
ours is uninhabited by human beings. That's obvious."
And that hit the nail right on the head.

❋ No man,
No woman

Inside the plantation house discovered by chance
among other diverse and refound distant things, great
irreversible deeds occurred and are still occurring in
our memories—reflections, flashes, flickers of lightning,
weighed in darkness. The mansion strangely retreating
behind range after range forever, along the edge of a
forest nurtured by some nameless river forbidden to the
imagination. Or perhaps it was not in a plantation house,
or at that undisclosed destination, or at such a distance?
It is impossible to know, now or ever.

But a child had ventured into the room at the end of
the veranda where there was a man who was featureless
though already "advanced in years," as the curious phrase
has it. He must have been the owner of the house. And
in that room—which was probably "the office," as such a

room usually is in large plantation houses with long, high verandas in that part of the country—there was a date on the calendar. The child could not read, but it is as if he were rereading it in a magazine: in the bright colors of the illustrations, and in their odor as well. For the odor is what lingers most vividly, fixing all the rest in our memory: the smell of the table, the desk, the drawer, and the rich red wood it was made of; that fragrance of what *never was again*. Now the man without features is trying to look like someone else—one of those old men, an uncle or acquaintance of ours, the one who spoke the least. It was later revealed, however, that he was no one but himself. Someone had merely addressed him, on that occasion, by a name with a similar sound; and the two persons, the familiar and the unfamiliar, are confused. Had someone else, then, entered the room? The Maiden, the image. It is the Maiden who reappears, lovely and unknowable. Her image hovers on the brink of such an extraordinary, wondrous light *that if someday I should discover what lies behind the word "peace," that gift would have come to me through her*. No, that date could not be the real one. Still, if it is a different date, it was imposed by a shifting trick of memory, for some good reason. Was it the Maiden who declared, in a voice unrelated to her, that the year was 1914? And the voice goes on correcting itself forever.

Was it really not so long and long ago, so still, so deep, so unreal as long as there are those still alive who might, perhaps, have shed light on where it had happened, where the Child had gone in these remote, extinguished years? Only now does a hard-won gleam of reminiscence appear, ever so slowly, as though at the end of a weary journey, piercing his consciousness. Only the light of the stars never reaches us in any other way.

Yet beyond the uttermost, what is, was, as far as the moonlight of the farthest distance which I know and vouch for. The house—rustic or seigniorial—with its invisible history sensed only in shadows and muted tints: the parapeted window, the landing on the staircase, the empty bunks of the slave quarters, the restless cattle? *If I can only remember I will be at rest; if I could find the link again: divine what is true and real, now past.* Is childhood a thing, a thing?

When the Maiden and the Youth were together an absorbed, enraptured look, different from all others, passed between them; both shed the same radiance. Each looked at the other with the look of birds surprised in song, trees on tiptoe, disconcerted clouds: as from blown-on ashes the splendor of flaring coals. They gazed at each other out of a noonday stillness, unknowing, unheeding of anything beyond themselves. But the Maiden was content to wait. But the Youth was eager. The Child, always near them, sought their eyes. *In the very preciseness with which other remembered scenes offer themselves from among a mingling of impressions, it may be that the astute malignancy of the dark part of us is incomprehensibly striving to deceive us, or at least to delay our scrutinizing any truth.* But the Child wished the two would never stop gazing at each other in that way. Eyes have unplumbed depths, like life.

How and why had the Child come to be sojourning in that house? Perhaps he had gone on a roundabout journey without any of his family. Had they expected his stay to be shorter than it was? For at first they all tried to keep him from seeing what was in a certain room, or even the section of the corridor off which it opened. *The doubt thus impressed upon the Child helps him to remember now.* The Maiden was the loveliest being ever seen; her beauty has no end. She might have been the princess in the castle tower. High around the tower, black eagles must have soared. The Man—old, quiet, unspeaking—must have been her father. The Man opposed no one; was he content, though silent? *The clouds are there not to be seen. Even a child knows enough, at times, to be wary of the narrow path we must tread between peace and anguish.*

Later on, either because they had changed their minds or because the Child's stay among them was to be a longer one, they let him know what was kept in that room. They let him see. And all it was was a woman. A little old woman—storied, historied—most unbelievably old. So old that she had shriveled to the tininess of a child, all wrinkled and faded: she would never walk any more, or even stand, and she hardly knew what went on about her, for she was no longer sound of mind. They no longer knew who she was, whose great-great-grandmother, any more than they could guess her unreckonable, incalculable age. She had crossed generations alone, although she was of our kind and feature. It was an immemorial tale; they had only the dimmest notion that she was related to them in some way. She was beyond comparisons. The Maiden tended her lovingly.

Faintly, faintly, the insistent effort must be made to remember something of the rain that fell, the plant that grew *in the past, through space,* the candelabra, the trunks, the chests, the flat round baskets, the gray lampshade in the shadows, the chapel, the pictures of saints, *like a piece of lace crumbling into fragments as it is unfolded,* the odors *never breathed again, suspended forests,* the glass picture stand, *forest and eyes, whitish islands,* people's voices, *extract and retain, revolve within me, bring into focus* the high beds of turned and polished wood, a pallet with a gilded headboard; *perhaps the things help most, it is the things that last the longest:* the long iron spit in the black woman's hand, the chocolate beater of jacaranda lying on the shelf beside cone-shaped cooking vessels, ewers, tin mugs. The Child was frightened and fled for refuge to the great dark kitchen, where women with heavy legs and feet laughed and talked.

Had the Maiden and the Youth gone to fetch him? He felt antipathy and rancor toward the Youth, of whom he was already jealous. The Maiden, all in black, exceedingly beautiful, tall, and snowy fair, like the maid of honor at a wedding; or did she belong in a theater? As she lifted the Child and carried him, he smelled blossoming green and rose, but gentler, graver than the smell of roses. The Youth laughed shortly. They soothed the Child, saying that no, the little old woman was not Death. She was not even dead. *On the contrary, she was life. There, in that one human being, life throbbed in silence, curled within and upon itself; it was only the heart, the spirit of life, that was waiting. That that woman should still be alive seemed an absurdity for which she was not even to blame.* Then the Youth was no longer laughing. The silent Man was also there, with his back turned. Standing, he told the fat black beads of his rosary.

They told the Child, and showed him, that the little Old Woman was not a ghost but a human being. Not knowing her name, they called her "Nenha." She lay so still in the middle of the high bed with its carved and polished posts, the pallet with the gilded headboard, that she almost disappeared among the bedclothes, inviolable in her exiguity, barely breathing. Every tiny wrinkle was the color of cider, and her wide-open eyes were blue-green. Hadn't she any eyelids? And yet, a tremor, a quiver, a little saliva in the withered pucker of her mouth, was sweetly incomprehensible. The Child asked, smiling: *"Has she gone to sleeping beautysleep?"* The Maiden kissed him. Life was the wind trying to blow out a lamp. The walking shadow of someone who is standing still.

The Maiden was content for everything to remain as it was. Did she have a fan? The Youth implored her, hung upon her with his eyes. The Maiden said to him: "You don't yet know how to suffer," and she trembled like the blue air. *I must remember. The past has come to me like a cloud, to be recognized; but I cannot decipher it.* They were in the big garden. Nenha, the tiny old woman, had been brought there too.

They carried her out to enjoy the sun, settled tinily in a basket that looked like a cradle. It was all so gay and gallant that the Child forgot himself and ran up: he wanted to play with her! The Maiden checked him gently, without reproaching him, and sat down among honeysuckle and rosemary, nonpareil. She looked at Nenha, long and intently, through the course of years, through other ages, she, too, an ancient child. She had covered Nenha with an antique shawl, so that the old woman's hands could not be seen. Only the funny little childlike bundle, the impalpable sleepy mumbling, sweetly ridiculous. They slipped soft food into her mouth. A fluttering of little smiles, a light plucking cough, and she was actually speaking (what she meant could scarcely be understood) in a semi-susurrus that was more discreet than the flickering of even the smallest white butterfly. Could the Maiden read her thoughts? She was asking for water. The Maiden brought the water, walking forward with the glass, full to the brim, in her two hands, smiling evenly, without spilling a single drop—and we thought she must have been born that way, with that brimming glass of water to be held until the hour of being unborn: from it nothing would be lost.

No, Nenha recognized none of them; withdrawn at the last, only thinking without intelligence of secrets condemned to oblivion, an enormous omission—an imperceptible heartbeat. *And yet, in the wandering of her eyes could be surprised the immanent dawn of beatitude: transcendent benignity, a ghostly good.* The Child asked: *"Is she right in the head?"* The Maiden's gaze deepened as the moon bleaches shadows. There was the sound of the big clippers pruning the rosetrees. The old Man was standing against the light, a very tall man. The Youth took the Maiden's hand, loving her. The Child shrank back into himself, staring at the ground, unhappily pouting.

The old Man wanted only to see the flowers, to be among them, to take care of them. He played with the flowers. *Fog closed in, and the dark; a great wall of fatigue. If I could only get my bearings! Like a stream coiling and circling up a mountain.* There was a string that could be rolled onto a little stick. The Maiden repeated so many things, so gently, to the Youth. *I need to recover, to undisremember, to think through—how can I say it— those torturing layers of forgetting. Just as I lived and changed, the past, too, has changed. If I can only find the thread again.* This was what the Youth and the Maiden were speaking of: the old Man, her father, in his last illness, when he would be at the point of death.

"Does he know yet?" asked the Youth, as the Maiden wiped the tiny old woman's sunken mouth with a delicate white handkerchief. *"He knows. But he doesn't know why!"* she said, shutting her eyes, stiff, still. The Youth bit off a curt: *"And who does know? And what good does it do, to know why we must die?"* Now it was the Maiden who took his hand.

I begin to remember, when I drowse off. How can it have been so wholly lost, the tradition of the name and person of that old, old Nenha, the ancestor preserved there by her kin? Before dying, someone still remembered that he did not remember: that she must have been the mother of another woman, and another, and another, back and back. Before coming to the plantation she had probably lived in a city or a town, in a certain house in a Square, where she had been cared for by some old-maid sisters. And they hardly counted. It had happened, long ago, that all of the breeding women in the family, the spinners and weavers, had died at almost the same time, one after the other, of the seven-day sickness, of child-bed fever; and after that, there was a break in the story as the men, wifeless, moved on and away. Little old Nenha, placed then in the care of strangers, visibly enduring beyond all the purlieus of ordinary life and old age, in perpetuity. *Then the fact dissolves. Memories are other distances. Things halted at the brink of a great dreamless sleep.* We are always growing, never knowing.

Observed from behind, the Youth argued with the

Maiden, gritting his teeth, unreserved in his speech, pressing at her gentle impassivity. She had said: ". . . *Wait,
until the hour of death."* Black-browed, nervous, the Youth
strained to understand her interdiction, for the Maiden
explained that it was not the death of her father nor of
old Nenha that she spoke, *"but our own."* As she said this
she smiled, deeply, as much like a flower as a woman
could be. Had she bound herself by a vow? No. But she
said: *"If I, if you love me . . . And how can we know
that this is the true love, the only one? Life's deceptive-
ness leads to so many mistakes. . . . Do you think you
could forget me, and even so, afterward, afterward, not
knowing, not willing it, go on loving? How can we be
sure?"* The Child trembled to hear the Maiden's reply,
wishing it unsaid. *The remembrance relost, the whole
scene is thrown into confusion: it is a bridge, a bridge—
but, at a certain moment, it seems to stop short. There is
a struggle with memory.* The bewildered Child has almost
lost his consciousness of self, as though he were no one,
or all were one person, one life: he, the Maiden, the
Youth, the old Man, and Nenha, the old woman—on
whom he fixed his eyes.

*Now you can see it—half-closing your eyes, as memory
demands: recognition, recollection of the picture; it clears,
becomes unclouded.* The desperate Youth, livid, rispid,
addressed the Maiden, clutching the rails of the garden
fence. He must have said that he was a simple man, too
sane of judgment to tempt God; that he meant to live an
ordinary life, using his own resources and following plain
roads! *What will happen now if the Maiden does not want
to hold him, if she will not agree?* The Maiden had tears
in her eyes but she still smiled, beautiful now in a new

way. She did not agree. She only looked at the Youth with boundless love. Then abruptly he turned away from her. And the Maiden knelt, bent over old Nenha's cradle, and wept and embraced her, embracing the incommutable, the immutable. So swiftly and totally did she set herself apart from the others that even the Child could not choose to stay with her and comfort her. Going against all that he felt, the Child went off with the Youth. The Youth suffered his presence, took him by the hand, and they walked away together.

The Youth walked stumblingly, feeling for the walls like a blind man. And they entered the room at the end of the veranda, the office. That writing desk made of red wood smelled so good, and the drawer too; the Child would have liked to keep the magazine with its colored pictures for himself but did not have the courage to ask for it. The Youth wrote a note—it was for the Maiden—and laid it down on the desk. What was in it no one knows or ever will know. The Maiden did not appear again. The Youth went away forever, turned wanderer, and the Child left with him to go back to his home. The Youth in his blue serge cape lifted the boy up to a seat in front of the saddle. They turned to look back when they were already some distance away; only the tall Man was standing in the doorway, his face unrecognizable, still waving farewell to them.

The journey must have been a long one, with that Youth who talked to the Child as to an equal, out of a necessity to seal with words what he had left behind. The Youth said: *"Will I be able to live without forgetting her until the great moment? Can it be that in my heart she is right?"* The Child did not answer, only thought loudly:

"*That is what I wonder!*" Oh, but he was angry with that Youth as though they were rivals—that Youth who was saying other things, things he would take no notice of. He asked whether he could ride on the croup instead of the pommel. He wanted not to be near the voice and heart of that Youth whom he detested. *There are times when the world suddenly shrinks, but then in a flash it swells too big again. We ought to wait for the third thought.* The Youth had stopped speaking. Beaten, driven, defeated, in confusion, he broke into sobs. Little by little, the Child too began to cry stealthily, and the horse whinnied. The Child felt then that if, somehow, he could will himself to love that Youth, then it would be in a way as if he were closer to the Maiden, so fair, so far, forever, alone. With that, he found himself at home. He was there.

I never heard again of the young man who had come with me, nor did I ever learn who he was. I noticed that my father had grown a mustache. Father was giving orders to two men who were building a new wall in the back yard. My mother kissed me, asked for news of everyone, and looked to see whether I had torn my clothes or lost any of the little holy medals from around my neck.

And I had to do something to relieve my feelings: I screamed at the two of them: "*You don't know anything, anything, you hear? You've forgotten everything you ever knew!*"

And they lowered their heads; I think they trembled.

For I did not know my parents—they were such strangers to me that I could never really know them, I; I?

❋ HOCUS

PSYCHOCUS

WHAT WENT ON on the night of our school play was Ooh.
It was enough to make your hair stand on end. As far as I
know, anyone knows, no one person ever did know exactly what happened. We think about it even now, years
afterward, but because of the suddenness more than the
confusion, and because of the confusion less than the
noise. After that night the fathers were about ready to put
a stop to those shows at the school. The one who never
could understand what had happened was our rehearser,
Dr. Crake, our professor of chorography and Brazilian history. He retired and went back to his home town, and if
he's still alive he must have gone beyond old age by now.
I wonder what ever became of the devil's little black boy,
Alfeu, the hunchback? Astramiro is an aviator now, and
Joaquincas a bookmaker and contiguous activities. I see

them both occasionally, and we talk over those crazy
times. The play we were putting on was a drama; it was
called *The Sons of Dr. Famous,* and it had only five acts.
Was its non-denouement the fault of us boys who were
chosen to act in it? Sometimes I think it was. Other times
that it wasn't. From the moment the monitor, Mr. Siqueira
("the Platypus"), solemn with mystery, called us together
after lunch during recess to hear the great news, we were
united in a pact of enthusiasm that never let up. There
were eleven of us, I mean twelve.

We were dazzled, you see. The Father Prefect com-
municated the solemn fact. Right there, with Dr. Crake
standing beside the Prefect, we said the Our Father and
three Hail Marys so that we might be granted the Pente-
costal tongues of fire. Then Dr. Crake, grasping the book
with the play in it, declaimed a summary that fired us all
up. Then every one of us had to read some lines from the
text, drawing out of himself the very finest voice he could
muster. We all read as if we were running a race. Zé Boné
was the only one of us who wasn't bashful about doing
his worst, and he made us laugh because he was such
a thoroughgoing nitwit. When Dr. Crake sent us away,
we remembered that our two most respected leaders—
Atahualpa, who was going to be *Dr. Famous,* and Darcy,
the *Captain Son*—were on the outs. But the two of them
agreed to make it up without our having to offer to act
as seconds. They made their peace, with Atahualpa giving Darcy a Transvaal stamp and Darcy giving Atahualpa
one from either Tasmania or China. Then they, the leaders, looked us over and gave us our orders: "Nobody tell
the others a word about the play!" It was agreed on and
settled and we took an oath. It took a few minutes for the

grand excitement of the thing to settle down in the corners of our heads. Except for Zé Boné, of course.

Zé Boné really did have a few screws loose. Without
ever stopping to talk or pay attention to anybody, he spent
every single recess tearing around imitating movies he
had seen: running and jumping like crazy from one side
of the schoolyard to the other; galloping like a horse, fir-
ing shots, robbing the stagecoach, yelling "Hands up!"
and then putting his hands up, and finally pretending to
be kissing somebody. He would act out the parts of the
hero, the heroine, the villains, and the sheriff, all at the
same time. He gave us plenty of laughs, the nincompoop.
Even so, they thought he was a better actor than I was;
the Prefect and Dr. Crake made up their minds that I was
too shy and ill at ease to do well in any of the scenes. It
was lucky for me that the Director happened to come in
just then and say flatly that since I was a diligent pupil
and applied myself and had the right kind of inflected
voice for a narrator, I would do very well as the prompter.
It made me laugh to see how the others treated me after
that. Joaquincas, who was going to take the role of the
Priest Son, gave me two new packs of cigarettes—two
different brands—and I gave him a fifty-reis piece and
half a roll I was keeping in my pocket. Then Darcy and
Atahualpa screwed up their courage and declared that
Zé Boné could never handle a part. But the Prefect repri-
manded us for our arrogance and reminded us that Zé
Boné's role, that of *A Policeman,* was one of the easiest
in the play, with hardly any lines for him to say. It was
no use for little Araújo, who was acting the part of *The
Other Policeman,* to make a nasty face: there were no
more opinions to be heard on the matter. Not that we

didn't drive Zé Boné to distraction with our cautious admonitions. Would he be able to keep from giving away the secret?

Then we had something else to worry about. What if the other pupils ganged up on us and tried to make us tell the story of the play? We were especially worried about two of the strongest boys, older boarders, who had not been chosen for the play because of their incorrigibly bad behavior! They were Dingdong and Hand-in-the-Jar, who was center forward on our team. Then someone on our side had an idea. All we had to do was invent some other story quick that we could fool the others into believing. And one of us would always have to stick close to Zé Boné to keep an eye on him.

We needen't have felt any misgivings. Zé Boné wasn't telling anybody anything. He couldn't even make sense out of the real plot except for a few of the funny parts and exciting incidents, which he shuffled into the movie plots he went on acting out at every recess with heroic, untiring agility. And Dingdong and Hand-in-the-Jar did not even mention the play, pretending it didn't matter to them. But the other story, the one we had made up, grew longer and longer, interminable in fact, with singular episodes that one or another of us would come up with: "the shooting," "the dueling train," "the 'dogface' mask," and especially "the bomb going off." The other pupils listened, liked it, and wanted more. Even black little Alfeu, the cook's son, who was lame, would drag himself over as fast as he could to hear, until the Platypus saw him and sent him away. To us it was already "our story," which we almost began to like better than the other one, the "real" story of the play—though I was too proud of my role of prompter not to learn by heart every single line of the real one. The only thing I wasn't very happy about was having to be hidden from the audience on the night of the great day under that bushel basket, the prompter's box, which we were not using during rehearsals.

"To act is to learn to live in true dignity, beyond frivolous sentiment," Dr. Crake exhorted us above his gray beard. Atahualpa—"Chesty"—and Darcy—"Spotty" —decided to give up those foolish nicknames. Some ladies were sewing the costumes we were going to wear: the cutaway coats for *Dr. Famous* and his *Friend,* the cassock for the *Priest Son,* the uniform for the *Captain Son.* We proposed to call each other by our stage names: Mesquita was "the Poet Son," Rutz "the Friend," Gil "the Man Who Knew the Secret," Nuno "the Police Sergeant." Dr. Crake dispelled possible embarrassment by decreeing that Niboca be called "Famulus" instead of "the Servant"; Astramiro was "the Redeemed Man" and not "the Criminal Son," and I was "the Master Prompter." "Remember: dignity and circumspection," our professor went on. "Art is long, life short . . . a preconization of the Greeks!" We began to worry that we might be deprived of our dream of glory. We made up our minds to be angels until the day of the show: not to smoke on the sly, not to talk in line or do the least little thing out of order, and to pay attention in class. Those of us who were not "Sons of Mary" petitioned to join the group. Joaquincas took communion every day, already visualizing himself as a holy priest. Every day after dinner we went upstairs for lengthy rehearsals, thus getting out of evening study hall under the double Cyclops eye of the Platypus; one more piece of good fortune which galled the other boys. "Take heart! On

your mettle! Let us persevere. Propriety and firmness.
Ad astra per aspera! Always ductile to my teachings . . ."
said Dr. Crake. We sighed after perfection, agonized over
the mise-en-scène. Except for Zé Boné, of course. He
marched in and saluted all right, but there was no way in
the world to get him to string two words together so that
they made sense. And the hour was drawing near, less
than two weeks away. Why not give the stupid fool's part
to somebody else? Dr. Crake would not hear of it: "My
beloved pupils, faint heart shall ne'er deter me from per-
sisting in preparing you for your roles!" Zé Boné, grasping
something of our professor's meaning from the tone of
his voice, drew himself up, clear-faced and contented.
Oh, we'd get even with him later, though! We'd teach him
a lesson after it was over! But not just then. All we felt
was expectancy. Constantly together in our remarkable
undertaking, we put off plans for our holidays and only
casually remembered our zeal for soccer.

If only it had not been for the time and the contre-
temps. Were the others making fun of us? They quoted,
with an air, lines we could not make head or tail of. They
said they already knew the real plot of the play and that
we were nothing but showoffs. Another complete version
was actually circulating; a well-put-together story at that,
but having nothing to do with the real one. Who had
spread it? Gamboa, a funny, inventive lad with the gift
of gab, who declared up and down that he knew the whole
truth. The dirty dog! We swore we'd beat him up, too,
after the show. The thing to do, then, was to counter
Gamboa's story, which was taking the wind out of our
sails. We repeated *our story* incessantly, in the sincerest
tone we could manage. The student body was divided into

partisans of one version or the other, who were constantly swinging over into the other camp, sometimes as often as several times a day. Were Dingdong and Hand-in-the-Jar leading the Gamboa faction?

"Let us deliver them up to the lofty justice of the Almighty . . ." lectured Joaquincas. "Hell's bells! Let me get my hands on them!" Darcy or Atahualpa bellowed out the sinful word. But "the reprobate, the improbate who brings evil fortune to my days . . ." was running wild. The Platypus said the play was robbing time from our lessons, which wasn't true, because we were going to get good marks on our exams anyway. But could this be?? Hand-in-the-Jar was getting together another soccer team because we hardly ever showed up for practice; oh misery! Was it worth the trouble of preventing Zé Boné from acting out his movies any more so as to see if he could get some sense into his head? Before we knew it some scenes from the play, the real thing, were being divulged. Was there a traitor among us? No: it was Alfeu. The little humpback could hardly walk straight on his wobbly, crooked legs, but he could slink quietly through corridors and up staircases, just like a lizard; and he had been sneaking up to listen to the rehearsals from behind the door. But we couldn't beat Alfeu, even after the show: he stole bread, sweets, chocolate, and other treats from the priests' kitchen for us. Would we have to pay him for his silence? Luckily, it was only for three more days. Dr. Crake had given up trying to stuff Zé Boné's part into him and had enjoined him to pantomime his lines and hold his tongue on stage. I had the toothache, my face threatened to swell up; or no, did it really not ache after all? Only two more days. What were Dingdong and Hand-in-the-Jar cooking up? Only a day and a half until the night before, and we trembled with excitement and longed for it, because that night was going to be the dress rehearsal.

"Come, take heart! Let us be unflagging in our zeal! . . ." Dr. Crake paced rapidly back and forth. The dress rehearsal was brilliant; everyone had his part on the tip of his tongue—to my disgust. Weren't they going to need the prompter? But then Jupiter's thunder broke over us. The Director had sat in on Act V. He was absent-minded and serious, regardless of whom he was speaking to. With no particular emphasis, he said we not only had it down pat, but too pat, without any spontaneous natural-ness or true breath of life. . . . He dismissed us. We were blank with consternation. And it was so late at night. Poor Dr. Crake, blanching to the roots of his beard, said haltingly: "My dear pupils . . . *Ad augusta per angusta* . . . Let us sleep," he groaned.

And who would have thought the following day, Sunday —the great day!—would be spent rehearsing, rehearsing, rehearsing—dear God, but everything was in an uproar and there weren't enough hours in the day: a long high mass, and honeybread and biscuits at breakfast, and us having to help get the theater ready, and the prompter's box freshly painted green, and a lot of girls and women arriving with our brand-new costumes nicely wrapped up. Meanwhile word went around that Dingdong and Hand-in-the-Jar were getting together some bullies to beat us up and start a ruckus. And outside visitors were arriving— parents and relatives—to see the play, and roaming through the school; and now some of the boys were saying that Dingdong and Hand-in-the-Jar's crowd, the Gamboa faction, were going to boo us!—and Dr. Crake sick all at

once with colic and a pain in his liver, and we were afraid
there wouldn't be any show, and the programs were all
ready, and even Alfeu had new clothes on, a sailor suit,
and his mother was making him use his crutches that
day, and Dr. Crake was up again and feeling all right with
his majestic black beard, and we had an early supper,
with bottles of lemon pop, and chicken, and meat pie, and
two kinds of dessert, until I couldn't eat any more; and
there was the Platypus coming in looking pleased—well,
I had been expecting some kind of funny business at the
very last minute; hadn't I spent the whole day with a
flea in my ear?

Silence. The Platypus went straight over to Atahualpa.
Atahualpa's uncle was at the gate—Atahualpa's father
was a Congressman and he was dying, in Rio de Janeiro.
Atahualpa would have to go by the train that was leaving
in two hours. But what about the play, the show? Atahualpa had already gone out with the Platypus to change
his clothes and pack his bag. But it was impossible not to
put on the play; it was to be a benefit performance. And
the only one who had learned all the parts and could be
Dr. Famous in Atahualpa's place . . . was me! Oh, and
what about the prompter? Doubt resolved: the prompter
would be—splendid!—Dr. Crake. Said and done.

Happy excitement—fear. The cutaway coat? The audience. The—half-hidden, nudging me—Alfeu! "Do you
want a swig?" of what he had swiped: a bottle of gin from
the Fathers' cellar—he said it would give me more courage. I didn't want any. What about the others? Zé Boné?
Alfeu didn't smile, he hissed. I didn't want to hear about
the others. I was being helped into my costume; the cutaway was just a little bit loose, not enough to make any

difference. The other boys probably didn't like having the ladies and girls putting rouge on their faces and lamp black on their eyes any better than I did—men didn't paint themselves! The momentous moment had come. The immense theater, the audience:—"They can't fit any more in!"—the multitude of heads, the din of people coming in and settling into their seats, noise, racket; oh, the lights. Dr. Crake, in a cutaway coat like ours, saying "Excelsior!" in a rather disconsolate voice. It was not the momentous moment; yes it was, no it wasn't. It was the hour on the hour. People seemed to be pushing us for no good reason. I was pushed out to the front. I could hear only the lights and laughter, but I could see much too much. Then silence.

I was standing there stock-still in my frock coat on the edge of the public world in front of me. But what did they want from me, what were they waiting for? My fellow actors were nudging me from behind; was this the time to play games? And oh!—all at once, in that swelling audience, I recognized each one in his place: Dingdong, Hand-in-the-Jar, Gamboa, the Platypus, Alfeu, the Director . . . oh!—and I had just remembered something awful, my lord, why hadn't anyone thought of that before? The way we were all lined up on the stage, with me in front, was called for in the program: Atahualpa was supposed to recite some verses in praise of our Patroness, the Virgin of Aparecida, and of our native land. But I didn't know those verses! Atahualpa was the only one who knew them, and Atahualpa was a long way off by now with his uncle, on the train, going to his father, who was on his deathbed . . . I didn't know the verses. I felt stiff and limp at the same time, sweated cold and hot, and I didn't know what to do; I stuttered uhuhuh and felt wildly at a loss.

The minute stopped. Thousands of people were laughing in my face. In the row where the Fathers were sitting I saw desperate gestures: orders, questions, signals explaining to me what I knew I didn't know and couldn't do. I shook my head and turned my pockets inside out to show that I didn't have the verses. I was being urged to do *something*. "Ring down the curtain!" I heard in the Prefect's voice. Dr. Crake, in his silly hole, made scraping sounds in his gullet. I made myself not look at the audience and spoke up loudly. I shouted tremulously: "Long live the Virgin and long live Brazil!"

Clapping resounded through the auditorium. "Ring down the curtain!" shouted the Prefect again from the wings. Because now it was really time for just *Dr. Famous* and his four sons to be on stage, and then the curtain would rise again for the first scene of the drama. ". . . Curtain!" But the curtain did not fall; it must have been stuck, because it never did come down. Total confusion. The actors who should have gone off the stage didn't go. We all advanced again without rhyme or reason, in a line like soldiers, or boobies. And then came the booing. It blared . . .

A booing like nobody ever heard. It was an ocean, a mob meowing, braying, bellowing, stamping. And we did nothing. There we were in formation like real soldiers, changing color and swallowing bile. "Attention! Come to order!" but even the priests could not put a stop to it. Dr. Crake was about to rise out of his prompter's box, but his nerve failed him and he ducked down again. We

stood staunchly, not budging a step, while the volley of
boos broke around us. The booing stopped. The booing
began again. We held our ground. "Zé Boné! Zé Boné!"
they shouted, after, during, and in the intervals between
the boos. "Zé Boné!"

That did it.

Zé Boné jumped forward, Zé Boné jumped to the side.
But this time it wasn't any western movie or rattle-brained
prank. Zé Boné began to act!

The booing came to a dead stop.

Zé Boné was acting—and acting well, smoothly, cleverly—to the amazement of all. He had a very important
role, only we couldn't tell what it was. But we didn't feel
like laughing, either. It was true. He was declaiming with
his whole being. Suddenly we realized that some of his
lines were from *Gamboa's story!* Loud applause.

We were flabbergasted. In a hot second I got my dan-
der up, and I think the others did too. Things couldn't
go on like that! We began to act out *the story we had made
up,* all of us at once. Zé Boné, too. It happened in the
nick of time. It was a glorious impulse—we couldn't have
planned it if we tried. More loud applause.

It was nonsense at first—just random humbuggery,
like a game of questions and answers. Dr. Crake loudly
and desperately whispered lines and cues, but we didn't
use many of them. The rest was light and agile words with
a shy admixture of gravity. Words from another climate.
I didn't know what I was going to say, but I said things
that were very well said, without clashing with the general tone. I know, because I was told afterward, that
everything took on a strong and beautiful meaning in
that unknown, frolicsome play, the best of all plays, the

play that no one had written and that could never be
acted out, ever again. I saw the audience lifted out of
itself, enjoying the spectacle in total silence. I saw that
we were no longer ourselves—that every one of us had
undergone a transformation. Dr. Crake must have wanted
to sink into the earth, if he hadn't already fainted inside
his proper prompter's box.

The Platypus and Alfeu shouted for encores. Even the
Director was laughing, just like Santa Claus. Oh, good
for us: each and every one of us was the hero, the other
actors, all the characters at once, personages personified.
And we were bravely going beyond real life, pushing on
in the most natural way in the world. And wasn't Zé Boné
the best of all? He sure was. Is. He's so good he shines
in the dark. Zé Boné!—and the performance quivers with
excitement. Success had come, lord knows how or from
where; but someone told me it was there—swore to it,
in fact.

But then—all of a sudden—was I afraid? Fear shook
me half out of my fine poetic frenzy. Wasn't that play
ever going to stop; didn't it have a beginning or an end?
No time seemed to have passed at all. How could we sen-
sibly put an end to it, then? But we had to. I tried hard
to break the spell I was under; but I couldn't do it, couldn't
swim out of the incessant, continuous current of the play.
They kept on clapping for us. Then I understood. Each of
us had transcended his own self, transported to unbelievable heights, knowing that he was really and truly alive.
And it was almost too good, too beautiful to bear—we were
borne on a cloud of myriadmarveled love, on the wings
of words: our own and those we heard the others say.
How could we stop?

Then, willing it and not willing it, and feeling myself unable to do it, I realized that there was only one thing to do. Only one way to interrupt the play, one way to break the chain, the river, the circle, the acting that would never stop of itself. Still talking, I walked to the front of the stage, to the very edge of the edge. I took one look, blinked, and turned a somersault. I toppled over on purpose and fell head over heels.

And I think the world came to an end.

It came to an end that night, anyway. Next day, when I was all right again and basking in glory during recess, Gamboa came up to me and said: "Hah, hah, eh? So my story was the real one, too, wasn't it?" I jumped on top of him and we fought a fierce fight.

THE THIRD BANK

OF THE RIVER

FATHER WAS a reliable, law-abiding, practical man, and
had been ever since he was a boy, as various people of
good sense testified when I asked them about him. I don't
remember that he seemed any crazier or even any moodier
than anyone else we knew. He just didn't talk much. It
was our mother who gave the orders and scolded us every
day—my sister, my brother, and me. Then one day my
father ordered a canoe for himself.

He took the matter very seriously. He had the canoe
made to his specifications of fine *vinhático* wood; a small
one, with a narrow board in the stern as though to leave
only enough room for the oarsman. Every bit of it was
hand-hewn of special strong wood carefully shaped, fit
to last in the water for twenty or thirty years. Mother
railed at the idea. How could a man who had never

fiddled away his time on such tricks propose to go fishing and hunting now, at his time of life? Father said nothing. Our house was closer to the river then than it is now, less than a quarter of a league away: there rolled the river, great, deep, and silent, always silent. It was so wide that you could hardly see the bank on the other side. I can never forget the day the canoe was ready.

Neither happy nor excited nor downcast, Father pulled his hat well down on his head and said one firm goodbye. He spoke not another word, took neither food nor other supplies, gave no parting advice. We thought Mother would have a fit, but she only blanched white, bit her lip, and said bitterly: "Go or stay; but if you go, don't you ever come back!" Father left his answer in suspense. He gave me a mild look and motioned me to go aside with him a few steps. I was afraid of Mother's anger, but I obeyed anyway, that time. The turn things had taken gave me the courage to ask: "Father, will you take me with you in that canoe?" But he just gave me a long look in return: gave me his blessing and motioned me to go back. I pretended to go, but instead turned off into a deep woodsy hollow to watch. Father stepped into the canoe, untied it, and began to paddle off. The canoe slipped away, a straight, even shadow like an alligator, slithery, long.

Our father never came back. He hadn't gone anywhere. He stuck to that stretch of the river, staying halfway across, always in the canoe, never to spring out of it, ever again. The strangeness of that truth was enough to dismay us all. What had never been before, was. Our relatives, the neighbors, and all our acquaintances met and took counsel together.

Mother, though, behaved very reasonably, with the result that everybody believed what no one wanted to put into words about our father: that he was mad. Only a few of them thought he might be keeping a vow, or—who could tell—maybe he was sick with some hideous disease like leprosy, and that was what had made him desert us to live out another life, close to his family and yet far enough away. The news spread by word of mouth, carried by people like travelers and those who lived along the banks of the river, who said of Father that he never landed at spit or cove, by day or by night, but always stuck to the river, lonely and outside human society. Finally, Mother and our relatives realized that the provisions he had hidden in the canoe must be getting low and thought that he would have to either land somewhere and go away from us for good—that seemed the most likely— or repent once and for all and come back home.

But they were wrong. I had made myself responsible for stealing a bit of food for him every day, an idea that had come to me the very first night, when the family had lighted bonfires on the riverbank and in their glare prayed and called out to Father. Every day from then on I went back to the river with a lump of hard brown sugar, some corn bread, or a bunch of bananas. Once, at the end of an hour of waiting that had dragged on and on, I caught sight of Father; he was way off, sitting in the bottom of the canoe as if suspended in the mirror smoothness of the river. He saw me, but he did not paddle over or make any sign. I held up the things to eat and then laid them in a hollowed-out rock in the river bluff, safe from any animals who might nose around and where they would be kept dry in rain or dew. Time after time, day after day, I did the same thing. Much later I had a surprise: Mother knew about my mission but, saying nothing and pretending she didn't, made it easier for me by putting out leftovers where I was sure to find them. Mother almost never showed what she was thinking.

Finally she sent for an uncle of ours, her brother, to help with the farm and with money matters, and she got a tutor for us children. She also arranged for the priest to come in his vestments to the river edge to exorcise Father and call upon him to desist from his sad obsession. Another time, she tried to scare Father by getting two soldiers to come. But none of it was any use. Father passed by at a distance, discernible only dimly through the river haze, going by in the canoe without ever letting anyone go close enough to touch him or even talk to him. The reporters who went out in a launch and tried to take his picture not long ago failed just like everybody else; Father crossed over to the other bank and steered the canoe into the thick swamp that goes on for miles, part reeds and part brush. Only he knew every hand's breadth of its blackness.

We just had to try to get used to it. But it was hard, and we never really managed. I'm judging by myself, of course. Whether I wanted to or not, my thoughts kept circling back and I found myself thinking of Father. The hard nub of it was that I couldn't begin to understand how he could hold out. Day and night, in bright sunshine or in rainstorms, in muggy heat or in the terrible cold spells in the middle of the year, without shelter or any protection but the old hat on his head, all through the weeks, and months, and years—he marked in no way the passing of his life. Father never landed, never put in at either shore or stopped at any of the river islands or sandbars; and he never again stepped onto grass or solid earth. It was true that in order to catch a little sleep he may have tied up the canoe at some concealed islet-spit. But he never lighted a fire on shore, had no lamp or candle, never struck a match again. He did no more than taste food; even the morsels he took from what we left for him along the roots of the fig tree or in the hollow stone at the foot of the cliff could not have been enough to keep him alive. Wasn't he ever sick? And what constant strength he must have had in his arms to maintain himself and the canoe ready for the piling up of the floodwaters where danger rolls on the great current, sweeping the bodies of dead animals and tree trunks downstream—frightening, threatening, crashing into him. And he never spoke another word to a living soul. We never talked about him, either. We only thought of him. Father could never be forgotten; and if, for short periods of time, we pretended to ourselves that we had forgotten, it was only to find ourselves roused suddenly by his memory, startled by it again and again.

My sister married; but Mother would have no festivities. He came into our minds whenever we ate something especially tasty, and when we were wrapped up snugly at night we thought of those bare unsheltered nights of cold, heavy rain, and Father with only his hand and maybe a calabash to bail the storm water out of the canoe. Every so often someone who knew us would remark that I was getting to look more and more like my father. But I knew that now he must be bushy-haired and bearded, his nails long, his body cadaverous and gaunt, burnt black by the sun, hairy as a beast and almost as naked, even with the pieces of clothing we left for him at intervals.

He never felt the need to know anything about us; had he no family affection? But out of love, love and respect, whenever I was praised for something good I had done, I would say: "It was Father who taught me how to do it that way." It wasn't true, exactly, but it was a truthful kind of lie. If he didn't remember us any more and didn't want to know how we were, why didn't he go farther up the river or down it, away to landing places where he would never be found? Only he knew. When my sister had a baby boy, she got it into her head that she must show Father his grandson. All of us went and stood on the bluff. The day was fine and my sister was wearing the white dress she had worn at her wedding. She lifted the baby up in her arms and her husband held a parasol over the two of them. We called and we waited. Our father didn't come. My sister wept; we all cried and hugged one another as we stood there.

After that my sister moved far away with her husband, and my brother decided to go live in the city. Times changed, with the slow swiftness of time. Mother went away too in the end, to live with my sister because she was growing old. I stayed on here, the only one of the family who was left. I could never think of marriage. I stayed where I was, burdened down with all life's cumbrous baggage. I knew Father needed me, as he wandered up and down on the river in the wilderness, even though he never gave a reason for what he had done. When at last I made up my mind that I had to know and finally made a firm attempt to find out, people told me rumor had it that Father might have given some explanation to the man who made the canoe for him. But now the builder was dead; and no one really knew or could recollect any more except that there had been some silly talk in the beginning, when the river was first swollen by such endless torrents of rain that everyone was afraid the world was coming to an end; then they had said that Father might have received a warning, like Noah, and so prepared the canoe ahead of time. I could half-recall the story. I could not even blame my father. And a few first white hairs began to appear on my head.

I was a man whose words were all sorrowful. Why did I feel so guilty, so guilty? Was it because of my father, who made his absence felt always, and because of the river-river-river, the river—flowing forever? I was suffering the onset of old age—this life of mine only postponed the inevitable. I had bed spells, pains in the belly, dizziness, twinges of rheumatism. And he? Why, oh why must he do what he did? He must suffer terribly. Old as he was, was he not bound to weaken in vigor sooner or later and let the canoe overturn or, when the river rose, let it drift unguided for hours downstream, until it finally went over the brink of the loud rushing fall of the cataract, with its wild boiling and death? My heart shrank. He was out there, with none of my easy security. I was guilty of I knew not what, filled with boundless sorrow in the deepest part of me. If I only knew—if only things were otherwise. And then, little by little, the idea came to me.

I could not even wait until next day. Was I crazy? No. In our house, the word *crazy* was not spoken, had never been spoken again in all those years; no one was condemned as crazy. Either no one is crazy, or everyone is.

I just went, taking along a sheet to wave with. I was very much in my right mind. I waited. After a long time he appeared; his indistinct bulk took form. He was there, sitting in the stern. He was there, a shout away. I called out several times. And I said the words which were making me say them, the sworn promise, the declaration. I had to force my voice to say: "Father, you're getting old, you've done your part. . . . You can come back now, you don't have to stay any longer. . . . You come back, and I'll do it, right now or whenever you want me to; it's what we both want. I'll take your place in the canoe!" And as I said it my heart beat to the rhythm of what was truest and best in me.

He heard me. He got to his feet. He dipped the paddle in the water, the bow pointed toward me; he had agreed. And suddenly I shuddered deeply, because he had lifted his arm and gestured a greeting—the first, after so many years. And I could not. . . . Panic-stricken, my hair standing on end, I ran, I fled, I left the place behind me in a mad headlong rush. For he seemed to be coming from the hereafter. And I am pleading, pleading, pleading for forgiveness.

I was struck by the solemn ice of fear, and I fell ill. I knew that no one ever heard of him again. Can I be a man, after having thus failed him? I am what never was —the unspeakable. I know it is too late for salvation now, but I am afraid to cut life short in the shallows of the world. At least, when death comes to the body, let them take me and put me in a wretched little canoe, and on the water that flows forever past its unending banks, let me go —down the river, away from the river, into the river— the river.

THE DAGOBÉ
BROTHERS

WHAT A TERRIBLE MISFORTUNE! It was the wake of
Damastor Dagobé, the eldest of four lawless, wicked
brothers. The house was not small, but it could hardly
hold all those who thought they should come to mourn.
Everyone tried to find a place near the corpse; everyone
was more or less afraid of the three survivors.

They were devils and ne'er-do-wells, those Dagobés,
who had lived in close discord, with no women in the
house and no other kinsmen, under the despotic chief-
tainship of the lately departed. Damastor had been the
worst of them, the ringleader, bully and master, who had
made his younger brothers live down to the same bad
reputation—"the young'uns," as he called them roughly.

Now, though, as long as he was in that unalive condition, he threatened no danger. All that was left, among the

lighted candles and a few flowers, was that ugly involun-
tary grimace, the piranha jaw, the crooked nose, and the
long list of wicked deeds. Under the gaze of the three
mourning survivors, however, one had to show respect;
it seemed best, somehow.

Coffee, burnt rum, and popcorn were passed around
every so often, as was the custom. There was a low, mo-
notonous hum of voices from groups of people who sat in
the darkness or were focused in the beam of lamps and
lanterns. Outside, night had closed in; it had rained a
little. At rare intervals someone would speak up more
loudly and then let his voice die down again, stricken,
realizing he had been careless. All in all, the ceremony
was like any other wake in those parts. Except that about
it was an air of calamity to come.

What had happened was this: A peaceful, honest nobody named Liojorge, liked by all his neighbors, was the
man who had sent Damastor Dagobé to join the dead on
the other side. Damastor, for no reason at all as far as
anyone knew, had threatened to cut off his ears. The
next time he saw Liojorge he took out after him at dagger point; but that quiet young man, who had managed
to obtain a blunderbuss, let him have it spang in the
chest, right over the heart. And that was the end of him.

After it was all over, people wondered why the brothers
had not yet taken their blood revenge and had made haste
to hold the wake and the funeral instead. And it really
was to be wondered at.

All the more because poor Liojorge was still in the
vicinity, at home all alone, resigned to the worst, without
the heart to make a move.

Who could understand such a thing? The surviving

Dagobés did the honors serenely, hardly skipping with
glee, of course, but seemingly in good enough spirits.
Derval, the baby of the family, was especially sociable,
solicitous of new arrivals as well as of those who were
already there: "Sorry we can't offer anything better . . ."
Doricão, who was now the eldest brother, was already
well into his role as the solemn successor of Damastor.
Like him he was corpulent, half leonine, half mulish; he
had the same protruding jaw and poisonous little eyes,
raised to heaven composedly as he declared: "God's looking after him!" The middle brother, Dismundo, a fine-
looking man, murmured with sentimental drawn-out de-
votion, gazing at the corpse on the table: "My good old
brother."

It was true that the deceased, who had been at least as
sordid a skinflint as he was tyrannical and cruel, had left
a fair sum of money in bills in a strongbox.

What was the point? They weren't fooling anybody.
They knew just how far they would go and what they
would do, only they weren't ready to do it yet. Those were
the ways of a wildcat. Soon they would act. They wanted
to take one step at a time, and they would not let anybody
hurry them. Blood for blood; but that one night, for those
few hours while they honored the departed, they could
lay their guns aside, falsely trustworthy. After the burial,
yes, then they would pounce on Liojorge and put an end
to him.

That was the gist of the comments spoken in corners,
with no idle movements of tongue or lips, in a whisper-
murmur, in the clouds of uneasiness and suspicion. For
those Dagobés, brutes shaken by fits of anger, but deceitful, too— men who knew how to keep the coals hot in the

pot—overlords as they were, were not the men to let bygones be bygones: their intentions were clear. For that
very reason they were unable to conceal a certain covert
contentment that was close to laughter. They were already
tasting blood. Whenever they could, they unostentatiously
grouped themselves at a windowsill for a low confabulation. And they drank. At no time did any of the three move
far from the others; what made them so cautious? Again
and again they were joined by some crony of theirs who
was more in their confidence than the others and who
brought news in a whisper.

Astonishing! People came and went as the night thinned
out, and always the subject of discussion was young
Liojorge, a criminal, but in legitimate self-defense, by
whose hand Damastor Dagobé had been given his traveling papers to the next world. Everyone at the wake knew
about it; little by little the word had been passed along.
Had Liojorge gone out of his mind, there by himself in
his own house? It was plain that he did not have the
gumption to seize his chance and escape. Not that it would
have done any good. Wherever he went, those three would
lay hands on him before very long. It was useless to resist, useless to run away, useless to do anything. He must
be crouching low, ashen-faced, perspiring with fear, without resources, courage, or weapons. It was none too soon
to pray for his soul! And yet . . .

Someone coming back from the spot gave the informa-
tion, the heart of the message, to the dead man's kin.
Liojorge, a stout young farmer, swore he hadn't meant to
kill any Christian man's brother. He had only pulled the
trigger at the very last minute to save himself, to fulfill
his disastrous fate! He had killed with all due respect.

And to prove it, he was willing to face them unarmed, to come in person and declare his total lack of guilt if they would act fair and square with him.

Pallid amazement. Had such a thing ever happened before? Liojorge must have gone mad with fright; he was already under sentence of death. Would he be even half brave enough to do it? To come—to jump out of the frying pan onto those hot coals? And it raised the gooseflesh to think of what everyone knew to be true: that in the presence of the murderer, the man he had killed would start bleeding again! These were certainly strange times. And another thing: there were no public authorities living anywhere near.

The guests looked sidelong at the Dagobés and their three blinks of the eye. Only: "All right," Dismundo said. And Derval: "He'll be welcome"—hospitable, doing the honors. Only severe, huge Doricão said nothing. He swelled with gravity. Fearfully, those standing near ventured to drink more burnt rum. It had rained again. A wake seems to go on too long, sometimes.

What they heard put a stop to their wondering aloud. Other ambassadors arrived. Were they trying to make peace or stir up trouble? Of all the unheard-of proposals! Liojorge was offering to help carry the coffin . . . did you hear that? A madman—and three wild beasts. As if what had already happened was not bad enough.

No one coud believe it when Doricão only made a noncommittal gesture as he took in the sense of the words. He spoke unemotionally, and his cold eyes widened. Well, all right, let him come—he said—after the coffin is closed. And so the plot was laid. You often see what you hadn't expected.

If, if, if? Everyone was waiting to see, a somber weight on his heart, fear spreading through his mind. Those were precarious hours. Day slowly dawned. Now it was morning. The dead man was stinking a little. Ugh.

The coffin was closed prosaically, without any prayers being said—the coffin, with its long lid. The Dagobés looked on with hatred in their eyes—hatred of Liojorge, people supposed, whispering. There was a general gloomurious stirring, a sound of: "He's coming. Right now," and other terse phrases.

Yes, he was coming. Everyone opened his eyes wide. Tall Liojorge, without a shred of good sense left in him. There was no animosity in the boy, he meant no insult. He said: "In Jesus' name!" to the three of them in a firm voice. And—that was all. Derval and Dismundo, plus Doricão, the devil himself in human form, who said nothing but: "Hum . . . hah!" What a scene.

They hoisted the coffin to carry it out, three men on each side, and motioned for Liojorge to take the handle in front, on the left. The Dagobés boxed him in, hate all around them. The procession left the house; the interminable had come to an end. A cluster of people, a small crowd, milled in the muddy street. The overeager walked in front, the prudent in the rear. All kept their eyes searchingly on the ground. At the very front the coffin jogged naturally along. And then came the wicked Dagobés. And Liojorge, surrounded. They walked on to the momentous burial.

Step-step, foot after foot. Whispering or silent, every soul in that intermingling understood the others, all equally hungry to question. There was no possible escape for Liojorge. He had to play his part as well as he could, even if his ears drooped. He was brave, and now there was no turning back. He might as well have been their servant. The coffin looked heavy. The three Dagobés were armed, capable of a sudden move. They had him in their gunsights; without seeing it, you could tell they did. Just then a fine rain began to fall, sopping faces and clothes. Liojorge—it was startling to see his dogged face, his subdued slavishness! Was he praying? He seemed not to be conscious of himself at all, but only of that fatal presence.

And now they all knew what would happen: once the coffin was lowered into the grave they would kill him at close range, before you could open your mouth and shut it again. The drizzle was letting up. Weren't they going to stop at the church? No, there was no priest in the village.

The procession moved on.

Now they entered the cemetery. "All come here to sleep," said the words on the gate. The shivering crowd stood in the mud at the edge of the hole in the ground, though many of the onlookers held a little back, prepared to run if they had to. There was a strong feeling of circumspectancy. Damastor, the once-and-no-more Dagobé, was given no farewell. With taut cords they lowered him deep into the earth and then earth was packed on top of him; the *pah, pah* of the spade was frightening to hear. What would happen now?

Young Liojorge waited; he was quietly self-contained. All he saw was seven handspans of earth in front of his face. His eyes were troubled, anxious—the brothers' plot. The silence was torturous. The other two, Dismundo and Derval, waited for Doricão. Suddenly he threw back his shoulders, as if only now had he noticed the other man among the crowd.

He looked at Liojorge briefly. Had he raised his hand to his gunbelt? No, it was those watching who mistakenly saw the gesture. Doricão only said abruptly: "Young fellow, go your way. Fact is, my departed brother was meaner than the devil."

He said the words softly, muttered them as if grudgingly. But he then turned to those present, thanking each one, and his brothers followed suit. You couldn't even be sure that they didn't smile, fleetingly. They shook the mud from their feet and wiped their spattered faces. Doricão, poised for swift flight, said his final words: "We're going away to live in the city." The funeral was over. And another rain began.

THE GIRL
FROM BEYOND

SHE LIVED behind the Sierra of Mim, in the middle of a swamp of clean, clear water, in a place called Fear-of-God. Her father, a small farmer, struggled along with a few cows and a patch of rice; her mother, a native of Urucúia, never put down her rosary, even when she was killing chickens or blessing out somebody. The little girl, named Maria—Nhinhinha, they called her—was always a little bit of a thing, but she had a big head and enormous eyes.

Not that she ever seemed to stare at things. She stayed quietly in her place, had no interest in rag dolls or other toys, but sat still, hardly moving, wherever she happened to be. "Nobody understands much of what she's talking about," said her bewildered father. It was not so much that she used strange words, although once in a while she would inquire, for instance: "Did she surego?"—but who or what she was talking about, no one was ever quite sure. Even more baffling was the oddness of her judgments about things, and the embellishments she might exclaim, with a burst of sudden laughter. Sometimes she told snatches of vague, absurd little stories: about a bee who flew up to a cloud; or a great many girls and boys sitting at a long, long table covered with cakes and candy, time without end; or the need to make a list of all the things people lost day after day.

Usually, though, Nhinhinha, who was not yet four years old, caused no one any trouble, and drew hardly any attention to herself except by her perfect calm, her immobility, and her silences. Nothing, no one, appeared to inspire her with any particular affection or distaste. When food was given to her, she sat with a leaf plate in her lap, eating first the meat, the egg, the cracklings, or whatever looked most appetizing and then consuming the rest— beans, cornmeal mush, rice, squash—with artistic slowness. Watching her perpetual imperturbability, one of us would suddenly exclaim in surprise: "Nhinhinha, what are you doing?" and she would reply in a long-drawn-out, mirthful, modulated voice: "I'm . . . ju-ust . . . do-o-oing," with empty spaces between the words. Could it be that she was just a tiny bit simpleminded?

Nothing intimidated her. Hearing her father ask her mother to brew some strong coffee, she would remark smilingly to herself: "Greedy boy . . . greedy boy . . ." and she was in the habit of addressing her mother as "Big girl . . . big girl . . ." which vexed both father and mother. In vain. Nhinhinha would only murmur: "Never mind . . . never mind," sensitive-soft, helpless as a flower. She would answer in the same way when summoned to see some new thing wonderful enough to excite adults and children alike. Events affected her not at all. She was subdued, but healthy and flourishing. No one had any real power over her; no one knew her likes and dislikes. How could she be punished? There was no way to chastise her. They would hardly have dared to strike her; there was no reason to do so, although the respect she felt toward mother and father seemed, rather, an odd sort of indulgence. And Nhinhinha was fond of me.

We talked together now and then. She loved the night in its heavy dark coat. "So full!" she would exclaim as she looked at the delible, superhuman stars, which she called "cheep-cheep stars." She repeated "Everything being born!" —her favorite exclamation—on many occasions, with the vouchsafing of a smile. And the air—she said that the air smelled of memories. "You can't see when the wind stops . . ." I remember her in the yard, in her little yellow dress. What she said was not always out of the ordinary; sometimes it was our ears that exaggerated what we heard. "Up so buzzard-high" was only "Up where the buzzard can't fly"—and her small finger would almost touch the sky. She would remark: "*Jabuticaba* fruit come-see-me!" and then sigh: "I want to go there." "Where?" "I don't know." Then she said: "The baby bird's gone away from singing." The birds had been singing, and as time slid by I thought she was no longer listening; then the singing bird stopped. "There's no more birdie," I told her. After that, Nhinhinha called the *sabiá*—the thrush— "Mrs. Birdie No-More." Some of her answers were longer than others: "Me? I'm making me homesick." At other times, when dead relatives were mentioned, she would laugh and say: "I'm going to visit them." I scolded her, advised her, said she was moonstruck. She eyed me mockingly, with perspective eyes: "Did he surego you?" I never saw Nhinhinha again.

I do know, however, that she began to work miracles at about that time.

It was neither her mother nor her father who discovered the sudden marvel, but Auntantônia. It happened one morning when Nhinhinha was sitting by herself staring at nothing in front of her. "I wish the toad would come." If they heard her at all, they thought she was spinning fairy tales, talking nonsense as usual. Auntantônia, out of habit, shook her finger at the child. But at that very moment the little creature hopped into the room, straight to the feet of Nhinhinha—not a toad with a bloated throat, but a beautiful mischievous frog from the verdant marsh, a green, green frog. Such a visitor had never entered the house before. Nhinhinha laughed: "He's weaving a magic spell." The others were amazed, struck dumb with surprise.

Several days later, with the same easy calm, she murmured: "I wish I had a corn cake with guava jam in it." And not half an hour later a stranger woman appeared, having come from a long way off, carrying the guava rolls wrapped in straw matting. Who could understand such a thing, or the new wonders that followed? Whatever she wanted was sure to happen at once. But she wanted very little, and always frivolous, careless things that made no difference one way or the other. When her mother was very sick, suffering pain for which there was no remedy, Nhinhinha could not be persuaded to tell them the cure. She only smiled, whispering her "Never mind . . . never mind," and refused to say any more. But she went slowly to her mother, hugged her, and kissed her warmly. The mother, staring at her little girl with astonished faith, was cured in a minute. And so they learned that Nhinhinha had more than one way of doing things.

The family decided to keep it a secret, so that malicious persons with ulterior motives, or the merely curious, would not stir up trouble, or the priests and the bishop try to take the child away to a solemn convent. No one would be told, not even the closest relatives. Auntantônia and Nhinhinha's parents themselves were not eager to talk about it. They felt an extraordinary fear of the thing. They hoped it was an illusion.

But what began to annoy the father, after a time, was that no sensible advantage was being taken of Nhinhinha's gift. A scorching drought had come; even the swamp threatened to dry up. They tried begging Nhinhinha to ask for rain. "But I can't, *ué*," she said, shaking her head. They insisted: they told her that otherwise there would be nothing left: no milk, rice, meat, candy, fruit, or molasses. "Never mind . . . never mind," she smiled gently, closing her eyes to their insistence and drifting into the sudden sleep of swallows.

Two days later she was willing to ask: she wanted a rainbow. It rained and soon the fairy arc appeared, shining in green and red, really a bright pink. Nhinhinha, no longer subdued, was overjoyed at the refreshing coolness that came at the end of the day. She did something they had never seen her do before: jumped and ran around the house and yard. "Did she see a little green bird?" her parents wondered aloud. As for the real birds, they sang like heralds from another kingdom. But that same day Auntantônia scolded the girl harshly, angrily, with such

rudeness that her mother and father were angry and surprised. Nhinhinha sat docilely down again, inexplicably
undisturbed, stiller than ever, thinking her green-bird
thoughts. Her father and mother whispered together con-
tentedly about how much help she was going to be to
them when she grew up and got some sense into her head,
as Providence of course willed that she should.

And then Nhinhinha fell sick and died. They say it was
because of the bad water in those parts. All acts of real
living take place too far away.

After that blow had fallen, suddenly every member of
the household began to suffer from one illness or another.
Mother, father, Auntantônia all realized that they might
as well be dead as half dead. It was heartbreaking to see
the mother fingering her rosary: instead of the Hail
Marys, she could only moan fiercely: "Big girl . . . big
girl," over and over. And the father's hands stroked the
little stool where Nhinhinha had so often sat, and which
would have broken under the weight of his man's body.

Now they had to send word to the village to build a
coffin and make preparations for the funeral, with virgins
and angels in the procession. Then Auntantônia plucked
up her courage: she had to tell them that on that day of
the rainbow, the rain, and the little bird, Nhinhinha had
spoken some wild foolishness, and that was why she had
scolded her. It was this: she had said she wanted a little
pink coffin trimmed in bright green . . . an evil omen!
And now, should they order the coffin made the way she
had wanted it?

Her father, in a shower of brusque tears, stormed
"No!" If he consented to that, it would seem as if he were
to blame; as if he were helping Nhinhinha to die.

But her mother did want it, and began to plead with the father. At the height of her sobs, however, her face grew serene and smiled a wide smile, a good smile, stopped short by a sudden thought. No, there was no need for them to order the coffin or to explain anything: it was bound to be exactly the way she had wanted it— rose-colored with green funeral trimmings—because it had to be! Because it would be another miracle, the last miracle of her little daughter in glory, Saint Nhinhinha.

☙ SORÔCO,

HIS MOTHER,

HIS DAUGHTER

THE RAILROAD CAR had been on the siding since the night
before. It had come with the express train from Rio, and
now it was there on the inside track near the station
platform. It was new and shiny—showier than an ordinary first-class passenger car. When you looked at it you
could see how different it was. It was divided into two
parts, and in one of the sections the windows were barred
like the windows in a jailhouse. It had come to take two
women far away, for good, on the train from the outback
which always went by at twelve forty-five.

A crowd had begun to gather around the car, just waiting. Not wanting to make a sad occasion of it, they talked
among themselves, each one trying to speak more reasonably than the others in order to show his wider practical
knowledge of the way things were. More and more people

arrived. There was a continuous stirring toward the end
of the platform, next to the corral where cattle were
loaded onto the train; just this side of the woodpiles was
the switchman's lookout house. Sorôco was going to bring
both women; he had agreed it had to be done. Sorôco's
mother was old, at least seventy. As for the daughter, she
was the only child he had. Sorôco was a widower. As far
as anyone knew he had no other kin at all.

It was the time of day when the sun is hottest, and the
people tried to stay in the shade of the cedar trees. The
railroad car looked like a big canoe, a ship on dry land.
When you looked at it, the heat shimmer in the air made
it seem out of kilter, turned up at each end. Its roof, like
a potbelly turned upside down, glittered blackly. The contraption looked as if it had been invented on some other
planet by someone without human feelings; you couldn't
possibly have imagined it, and you couldn't get used to
seeing it; and it didn't belong to the world you knew. It
was going to take the women to a town called Barbacena,
a long way off. Places are farther away to a poor man.

The stationmaster came up in his yellow uniform,
carrying a black-covered book and some little green and
red flags under his arm. "Go see if they've put fresh water
in the car," he ordered. Then the brakeman began to move
the coupling hoses. Someone called out: "Here they
come!" and pointed to the lower street where Sorôco lived.
He was a burly man with a thick body, a large face, and
a stringy, stained yellow beard, who usually wore only
sandals on his feet. Children were afraid of Sorôco, especially of his voice, which, when he spoke at all, was at
first very rough and then faded out. Here they came, with
a whole retinue.

They stopped and stood still. The girl—the daughter—
had started to sing, lifting her arms high. The song
straggled uncertainly; it was off-key and the words were
nonsense. The girl raised her eyes to heaven like a saint
or a woman possessed. She was decked out in tomfool-
eries, a wonder to behold, with a cap made of varicolored
pieces of cloth and paper on her scattered hair. Her figure
bulged with its wild mixture of clothing, ribbons dan-
gling, sashes tied on, and all sorts of gewgaws: pure craziness. The old woman, in a plain black dress with a black
fichu, shook her head gently back and forth. So different,
the two women were alike.

Soroco gave an arm to each of them, one on each side,
as if they were going into church for a wedding. It was a
sad mockery, though, more like a funeral. The crowd
stayed a little apart, not wanting to look too closely at
those wild ways and absurdities for fear of laughing, and
also because of Soroco; it would have seemed like a lack
of consideration. Today, in his boots, his overcoat, his big
hat—all his raggedy best which he had put on—he
seemed diminished from his usual self, bewildered, almost humble. Everyone paid his respectful condolences,
and Soroco said: "God repay you for your trouble."

What the people said to one another was that Soroco
had been wonderfully patient and certainly wouldn't miss
the poor disturbed things; it would be a mercy to have
them gone. There was no cure for what was wrong with
them, and they weren't coming back, ever again. Soroco
had gone through so much and borne so many misfortunes; living with the two of them had been a struggle for
him. And then they had gotten worse as the years went
by; he had not been able to manage any longer and had

had to ask for help. The authorities had come to his aid
and made all the arrangements, free of charge. The government was paying for everything and had sent the
special railroad car. That was how it happened that the
two women were going to be put away in the madhouse.
That was what was coming.

Suddenly the old woman let go of Sorôco's arm and
went and sat down on the steps of the car. "She's harmless, Mr. Stationmaster"—Sorôco's voice was very soft—
"but she doesn't come when you call her." Then the girl
started to sing again, turning first to the crowd, then to
the sky, her face in ecstatic repose. It was not that she
wanted to make a show of herself; she was acting out
grand, impossible scenes of long ago. But the townspeople
saw the old woman look at her with an ancient, charmed
foreboding—an extremity of love. And, starting out softly,
her voice growing stronger, she began to sing too, following the other woman in the same song that no one
could understand. Now they were singing together, on
and on.

It was about time for the train to come, and they had
to make an end to the preliminaries and get the two
women into the car with its windows crisscrossed with
bars. It was done in a twinkling, with no farewells—
which the two women would not have been able to understand anyway. Into the coach went the people who were
going along to do for them on the long journey; the
bustling, cheerful Nenêgo and Blessed José, who was a
very reliable person. Those two could be trusted to keep
an eye on the women, whatever happened. Some young
lads climbed into the car, carrying the bundles and suit-
cases, and the meat—there were plenty of eatables, they

wouldn't lack for a thing—and wrapped-up loaves of bread. Last of all, Nenêgo appeared on the platform, gesturing to show that everything was all right. The two women were not going to make any trouble.

Now all that could be heard was the women's lively singing, that shrill, distracted chanting which symbolized the great vicissitudes of this life, which can hurt you for any reason at all, anywhere, early or late.

Sorôco.

If only it would end. The train was coming. The engine maneuvered to pick up the car on the siding. The train blew its whistle and glided loudly away and left, exactly as it always did.

Sorôco did not wait for it to disappear. He never looked at it, but stood with his hat in his hand and his square beard, deaf—that was what seemed so pitiful; the plain open sadness of the man, who seemed unable to say even a few words. He was suffering the way of things, in a hole with no way to climb out of it, bearing the weight uncomplainingly, setting a good example. They told him: "That's the way the world is." All of them stared respectfully, their eyes moist. Suddenly everyone loved Sorôco.

He shook himself awkwardly, with a now-it's-over-with sort of shrug, as if he were worn out, not important any longer, and then turned to go. He started off for home as though on a journey that was too long to be measured.

But then he stopped. He hesitated in a peculiar way, as if he were no longer sure of his old self and had lost his identity. It was as if he were pure spirit, beyond reason. And then something happened that could not have been foreseen; who would ever have thought of it? All at once he burst out singing, high and strong, but only for himself

—and it was the same meaningless song the two women had sung, over and over. He sang on and on.

The crowd stiffened and was nonplussed—but only for a second. A whole crowd . . . and then, with no agreement beforehand, without anyone's realizing what he was doing, all, with one voice, in their pity for Sorôco, began to accompany that nonsense song. And how loud their voices were! They all followed Sorôco, singing, singing, with those farthest behind almost running to catch up, but every one of them singing. It was a thing none of us will ever forget. There was never anything like it.

Now we were really taking Sorôco home. We were going with him, as far as that song could go.

☸ **N**OTORIOUS

IT WAS FUNNY the way it happened. Who would have expected a thing like that with no head or tail to it? I was indoors and the settlement was quiet. When the hoofbeats stopped at my door, I went to the window.

It was a group of men on horseback. That is, when I took a closer look I saw one rider, all fitted out, right at my door, and three others bunched up together. I saw it all at a glance, and it was mighty unusual. Took a grip on my nerves. That one rider—man oh man, he was a mean-looking cuss. I know how a man's face can brand him for life, and that man was born to die fighting. He gave me a dry, short, heavy hello. He was riding a tall sorrel horse, well harnessed and saddled and shod, and sweating. And I began to be afraid something bad was in store for me.

None of them dismounted. The others, the down-in-the-mouth threesome, glanced my way once and didn't look again. They appeared to be a scared, cowed, hangdog lot. Uneasy, as if they weren't there of their own free will; that was it. Matter of fact, it looked as though they took orders from the shrewd-looking fellow. He pointed with a sort of scornful half-wave of his hand, and they went where he pointed. You see, the front of the house was set back a few yards from the street and there was a fence along each side, making a safe kind of a corner; and the man made the others go back where they wouldn't be seen and barred their getaway at the same time. They couldn't have moved very fast anyhow, with their horses all squeezed together like that. He had noticed everything and taken advantage of the lay of the land. The other three might have been his prisoners instead of his followers. The way that fellow was acting, he was bound to be a wild man from the bush, a killer right down to his liver and lights. I could see it was no use to put on a smile and let him know I was afraid. I didn't have a gun within reach, and even if I'd had one it wouldn't have been much use. He'd have blown me into a heap of dust quick as dotting an i. Fear is knowing how ignorant you are when you're in a jam. Fear with a capital F was screeching around inside me. I called out to him to dismount and come inside.

No, he wouldn't, although he knew it was the custom. Kept his hat on, too. You could see he was resting in the saddle now—letting himself hang loose so he could think better. When I asked he said no, he wasn't sick; hadn't come for a prescription or an examination. He spaced out the words, making his voice sound calm; he talked like the backlanders who live around the São Francisco River.

I know a thing or two about that kind of fighting man who doesn't go around boasting and talking big. Mean as the devil, but keeps the meanness bottled up and then lets fly all of a sudden because of a yes-you-are-no-you-ain't. I began to steady my wits, slow and careful. He said: "I came here to ask your 'pinion 'bout a certain matter . . ."

He beetled his brow. It got me worried again; that black stare, and the cannibal cut of him. He stopped frowning, though, and almost smiled for a second. Then he jumped off his horse, handy and light and sudden. Did he think better manners would get him a better answer; was it canniness? He kept the end of the bridle around his wrist; the sorrel was a peaceable animal. The hat was still on his head; he was pretty uncouth after all. And his eyes didn't give away a thing. He was ready for anything, that was plain. He had his gun with him, all clean and polished. You could sense the weight of it in his belt, which he wore low so as to have the revolver handy, at just the right height. And he kept his right arm hanging down, loose-like. The saddle caught my eye—a rounded, high-pommeled saddle from Urucúia of a kind you don't see around here very often, at least not so well made. All those things belonged to a fighting man. That one had blood on his mind. He was short but hard and stocky, like a tree trunk. His violence might break out at any minute. If only he'd have come on in and taken a cup of coffee, I'd have felt a lot better about him. But his staying outside that way, without company manners and where all the walls had ears—well, anybody would have been worried, not knowing what to expect.

"You don't know me, I reckon. Damázio Siqueira. Just came down from the Sierra."

That gave me a fright. Damázio—who hadn't heard of

Damázio? The stories of his ferocity had traveled for
miles around. He had dozens of deaths on his conscience.
A very dangerous man. They also said, and it might have
been true, that he had calmed down some in the last few
years, that he steered clear of trouble when he could. But
for all that, who's willing to put his trust in the truce of
a panther? And there he was, a hand's span away, right
in front of my nose! He went on:

"I want you to know that a government fellow's been
sniffing around up there in the hills lately, the kind of
young fellow that talks a mite too much. . . . Well, I'm
on the outs with him. . . . Now I don't want any fuss
with the government, 'cause my health ain't so good and
I ain't as young as I used to be. . . . A lot of folks think
that young fellow ain't got an awful lot of sense. . . ."

All of a sudden he pulled up short, as if he was sorry
he had started out that way, spilling his story right off. He
thought and thought, hangdog head hanging down. Then
he made up his mind and his face lighted up. You couldn't
call it laughing, not with those cruel teeth. He didn't look
at me, either; not unless it was out of the corner of his
eye. There was a prideful worry pounding in him. He
commenced talking again.

It was random kind of talk; he spoke about different
people and about things in the Sierra, in São Ão, all kinds
of subjects in no kind of order. Listening to that talk of
his was like getting wound up in a spiderweb. I had to
try and understand every little inflection of his voice and
every silence too, to try to see what he was leading up to.
He was playing close to his chest. Yes, he was a sly one,
it wasn't easy to puzzle out what he was driving at. And
then, bang:

"And now will you do me a good turn? Will you learn me the right meaning of *northerious* . . . *motorious* . . . *mastorious* . . . *nosterrious* . . . ?"

The words came in a rush between clenched teeth, with a thunderclap of dry laughter. But then he made a gesture that expressed all his exaggerated, primitive rudeness. He waved away my answer, not wanting me to give it right away. And here another frightful thought made me dizzy: maybe someone had wanted to stir up trouble by inventing things, saying I had insulted the man, laying it all at my doorstep. In that case, what could be more natural than for him to hunt me up so that he could have his fatal revenge on me, face to face?

"I want you to know all I came down for today, six leagues without stopping, straight into town, was to ask you that question and get a straight answer."

It was a serious business, all right. I was frozen to the spot.

"Up there, and on the road on the way down, there wasn't nobody could tell me, nobody had the real thing— I mean that book that has all the words in it. . . . Folks give you a crooked answer, pretendin' to be less ignorant than what they are. . . . Maybe the padre over in São Ão could have told me, but I don't get along so good with priests, they always try to holytalk you. . . . Well, never mind that. Now if you'll kindly tell me, on the level, man to man: what does it mean, that word I asked you just now?"

Easy. Shall I tell him? He had me on the point of his knife.

"Notorious?"

"Yes, sir"—and he repeated the term again, loudly,

several times, his face reddening with anger, his voice out of focus. He was looking at me now, inquiringly, threateningly, closing in on me. I had to show my hand. "Notorious?" I thought about how I could lead up to it. What I needed right then was a breathing spell to think it over. Casting around for help, I glanced at the three men on horseback, wrapped up in themselves all that time, mute as mummies. But Damázio was impatient:

"Go on and tell me. Don't pay any mind to them. They're from up in the hills. I only brought 'em along as witnesses."

I was in a tight spot and had to work myself out of it somehow. The fellow wanted the gist and the gospel.

" 'Notorious' isn't any offense; it means 'celebrated,' 'famous,' 'remarkable' . . ."

"Don't think bad of me 'cause I'm thick-headed and don't understand. Just tell me this: Is it abuse? Is it spite? Is it a cussword? A joke? An insult?"

"Neither insult nor injury. Those are neutral expressions, with a different meaning."

"Well, what is it then, in poor man's talk and weekday language?"

" 'Notorious'? Well. It means: 'important,' 'deserving of praise and respect' . . ."

"Will you swear by the peace of both our mothers' souls, with your hand on the Good Book?"

Would I swear! I would have pledged my own beard. I answered him, as sincere as the devil:

"Look here. Just as I'm standing before you now, with —ahem—all my advantages, I only wish I were notorious, really notorious, as notorious as possible!"

"Well, now!" he burst out triumphantly.

He jumped into the saddle as if he had been on springs. He was himself again, no longer thirsty for vengeance. The bonfire had been put out. He beamed, a new man, and informed his three companions: "You can go now, friends. You all heard that good explaining"—and they lit out as fast as they could. Only then did Damázio come right up to the windowsill; yes, a glass of water would taste good. He remarked: "There ain't nobody in this world who's more of a he-man than a fellow with an education!"

Was he clouding over again for no reason? He said: "I don't know. I'm thinkin' it might be better for that government fellow to move on after all, I don't know. . . ." But then he smiled, no longer uneasy in his mind, and added: "You get all riled up over some piece of foolishness, some little doubt . . . just addle your brains over nothing . . ."

He thanked me and shook my hand. He'd come into the house next time. Oh, yes. He spurred the sorrel and trotted off, no longer thinking about what had brought him. That confounded word would give him something to feel good about for a long time to come.

❖ TREETOPS

IT WAS once upon another time. And again the little boy was on his way to the place where many thousands of men were building the great city. But this time he was traveling along with his uncle, and the departure was arduous. He had stumbled bewilderedly into the plane, a lump of something like weariness rolling around in his stomach; he only pretended to smile when he was spoken to. He knew that his mother was ill. That was why they were sending him away, surely for a long time, surely because they had to. That was why they had wanted him to bring his toys. His aunt had handed him his favorite, lucky toy: a little monkey doll with brown trousers and a red hat with a tall feather, whose face was on the table in his bedroom. If it could have moved and lived like a person, it would have been more mischievous and full of tricks than anybody. The boy became more afraid the more kindly the grownups treated him. If his uncle jokingly urged him to peer out the window or choose some magazines to look at, he knew that Uncle was not entirely sincere. And other things frightened him, too. If he thought only of his mother, he would cry. Mother and sorrow would not fit in the space of the same instant; one was the other turned inside out—it was horrible, impossible. He could not understand it himself; it was all mixed up in his little head. It was like this: something bigger than everything else in the world might happen, was going to happen.

It was not even worth looking at the far-drifting, superimposed clouds that were moving in different directions. And didn't all of them, even the pilot, seem sad, only pretending to be normally cheerful? Uncle was wiping his glasses on his green necktie. Surely he would not have put on such a pretty tie if Mother was in danger. The boy conceived a feeling of remorse at having the little monkey doll in his pocket, so funny and always the same, just a toy, with the tall feather in its little red hat. Should he throw it away? No; the monkey in the brown trousers was his little companion, and after all, did not deserve to be treated so badly. He only took off the little hat with the plume and threw it away; now it was no more. And the boy was deep inside of himself, in some little corner of his being. He was a long way back. The poor little boy sitting down.

How he did want to sleep. People ought to be able to stop being awake whenever they needed to and drop safely and soundly off to sleep. But it wouldn't work. He had to open his eyes again even wider, to look at the clouds experimenting with ephemeral sculptures. Uncle glanced at his watch. And what would happen when they got there? Everything, all-the-time, was more or less the same, things and other things like them. But people were not. Doesn't life ever stop so that people can live on an even keel and have time to straighten themselves out? Even the little hatless monkey would know, in the same way as he did, the size of those trees in the forest, beside the land on which the house had been built. Poor little monkey, so small, so lonely, so motherless; he held it inside his pocket, and the monkey seemed to be thanking him and crying down there in the dark.

But Mother was only a momentary happiness. If he had known that she was going to get sick one day, he would always have stayed near her, looking at her hard, and really conscious that he was with her and looking at her with all his might. He would never even have played with anything else but would have stayed close to her side, without being separated from her for even the space of a breath, not wanting anything to change. Just as he was now, in the heart of his thoughts. He felt that he was with her even more closely than if they had been together.

The airplane unceasingly crossed the enormous brightness, flying its seemingly motionless flight. But certainly black fish were passing them in the air beyond those clouds, hump-backed and clawed. The boy suffered, was suppressed. What if the plane were hanging in one place as it flew?—and it flew backward, farther and farther, and he was with his mother, in a way that he had never imagined he could be.

The Bird Appears

In the unchanged house, which was just as it had always
been with the trees around and behind it, everyone began
to treat him with exaggerated care. They said it was a
shame there were no other children there. If there had
been, he would have given them his toys; he did not ever
want to play again. While you were playing and not paying attention, bad things were laying traps for you, getting ready to happen; they lay in wait for you behind the
doors.

He felt no desire to go out in the jeep with Uncle,
either, just to see dust, earth, people. When he did go, he
held on tight with his eyes shut; Uncle told him he
shouldn't clutch so hard but let his body relax, joggling
to and fro with the jouncing of the jeep. If he got sick,
very sick, where would he be: farther from his mother, or
nearer to her? He bit on his heart. He would not even talk
to the little monkey doll. That whole day was good for
only one thing: to spread his tiredness more thinly.

Even when night fell he could not get to sleep. The air
in that place was very cold, but thin. When he lay down
the boy felt frightened; his heart thudded. Mother, that
is . . . And he couldn't sleep just then, because of her.
The stillness, the darkness, the house, the night—all of it
walked slowly toward the next day. Even if you wanted
it to, nothing would stop or go back to what you already
knew and loved. He was all alone in the room. But the
little monkey doll's place was no longer on the bedtable: it
was the comrade on the pillow, lying belly up with its
legs stretched out. Uncle's bedroom next door was sepa-

rated from his own by a thin wooden wall. Uncle was snoring. So was the little monkey, almost, like a very old little boy. What if they were all stealing something from the night?

And when day broke, in the no-longer-sleeping and not-yet-waking, the boy received a flash of insight—a sweet, free breath. It was as if he were watching someone else remembering the verities; almost a kind of film of thoughts previously unknown to him, as if he were able to copy the ideas of great men in his own mind. Ideas that faded into shreds.

But within that radiance, soul and mind both knew that you can never wholly apprehend the events that are beautiful and good. Sometimes they happened so swiftly and unexpectedly that you weren't prepared for them. Or you had looked forward to them, and then they didn't taste so sweet after all, but were only a rude approximation. Or there were awful things along with them, on both sides of them, nothing clean and clear anywhere. Or something was missing which had happened on other occasions and would have made this second event perfect. Or else you knew, even as they happened, that they were on the way to ending, gnawed by the hours, falling to pieces. . . . The boy could stay in bed no longer. Already up and dressed, he picked up the monkey and put it in his pocket. He was hungry.

The porch formed a passageway between the little house lot and the jungle surrounding it, and the wide outside—that dark country under quick forays of fog, ice-cold, pearled with dew: stretching out of sight, to the rim of the eastern sky, on the far edge of the horizon. The sun had still not appeared. But there was a brightness touching the treetops with gold. The tall trees beyond the clearing were even greener than the grass the dew had washed. It was almost day—and from it all came a perfume and the chirping of birds. Someone brought coffee from the kitchen.

And—"Psst!"—someone pointed. A toucan had flown to one of the trees on noiseless horizontal wingbeats. He was so near! The high blue, the fronds, the shining bands of yellow and the tender shades of red on the bird, when it alighted. Such a sight: so big, in such gala dress, its beak like a parasitic flower. It leaped from branch to branch, feasting from the laden tree. All the light belonged to the bird and was sprinkled with its colors as it sprang into the middle of the air, preposterously free, splendidly suspended. *Tuk-tuk* in the treetop, among the berries . . . Then it cleaned its beak on a branch. And the wide-eyed boy, unable to clasp the foreshortened moment to himself, could only count one-two-three in silence. No one spoke. Not even Uncle. Uncle was enjoying it too; he wiped his glasses. The toucan paused, hearing other birds—its babies, perhaps—from the direction of the woods. Its great beak turned skyward, it let out one or two of those rusty-sounding toucan cries: *"Creeh!"* . . . and the boy was on the verge of tears. Just then the cocks crowed. The boy remembered, remembering nothing. His eyelashes were wet.

And then the toucan flew in straight, slow flight—it flew away, shoo, shoo!—mirable, grandly dressed, all hovering color; dream stuff. But before his eyes were cool, someone was already pointing to the other side of the world. There the sun was about to come up, in the region of the morning star. At the edge of the fields that were like a dark, low wall, there broke through at one point a golden rhombus with jagged edges. There swung upward softly, in light, unhurried steps, the half-sun, the smooth disk, the sun, the light complete. Now it was a golden ball hung by a thread on azure. Uncle glanced at his watch. All that time the boy had not made a sound. His gaze seized on every syllable of the horizon.

But he was unable to reconcile that dizzying moment with the present memory of his mother—cured, oh no, not sick any more, just as happy as she would have to be if she were there. Nor with the momentary idea of taking his little comrade, the monkey doll, out of his pocket so that it too could see the toucan: the little red god clapping its hands, its beak upright. It was as if it hung motionless during each separate moment of its flight, but in that infinitesimal, impossible point, not in air—now, eternally, and forever.

The Bird's Task

And so the boy, in the dejected middle of the day, struggled with what he rejected in himself. He could not bear to see things in their raw state, as they really are, as they always tend to become: heavier, thingier—when you let yourself look at them without taking precautions. He was afraid to ask for news; did he fear for his mother, lost in the evil mirage of illness? However reluctant he might be to go on, he could not think backward. If he wanted to imagine his mother as being ill, unwell, he could not fit his thoughts together; everything was erased from his head. Mother was just Mother; that was all.

He waited, though, for perfect beauty. There was the toucan—flawless—in flight and rest and flight. Anew each morning, returning always to that high-crowned tree, of the kind that is, in fact, called "toucan tree." Taking its golden pause at daybreak. Each dawn, at the same time, the punctual, noisy toucan . . . come, come . . . in easy flight, as if at rest, drawn softly on the air, like a little red boat lazily shaking its sails as if it were being pulled along like a toy; as horizontally as a duckling gliding forward over the light of golden water.

After that enchantment, he had to begin the common body of the day. The day that belonged to other people, not to him. The jouncings of the jeep shaped the next happening. His mother had always warned him to be careful of his nice clothes, but this place defeated all his efforts. Even the little monkey doll, though it was always kept in his pocket, got sweaty and dusty. The thousand, thousand men labored mightily, building the great city.

But the toucan infallibly came just as dawn was being painted, and all knew him. The coming had begun more than a month before. First there had appeared a band of about thirty of the loud-voiced birds, but in midmorning, between ten and eleven o'clock. Only that one had stayed on to return at first daylight each morning. With his heavy eyes dizzy with sleep, the little monkey doll in his pocket, the boy rose hastily and went down to the porch, eager to love.

His uncle talked to him with excessive amiability and painful awkwardness. They went out—to see what was going on. The dust clouded everything. Someday the monkey doll ought to have another little hat with a tall feather;

but this time a green one, the color of that remarkable tie that his uncle was not wearing now because he was in his shirtsleeves. At every given moment it was as though a part of the boy were being pushed forward, against his will. The jeep ran over roads which went nowhere and were always in the process of being built. But the boy, in the strong core of his heart, swore only that his mother had to get well, that she had to be saved!

He waited for the toucan to alight on the tree on time, on the dot of six twenty each morning; it always perched on the main mast of the toucan tree and pecked at the fruit for just those ten minutes, gnawed away and consumed. Then it flew off, always in that other-direction, just before the dropped half-instant in which the red sphere of the sun rolled up from the plain; the sun rose at six thirty. Uncle timed it by his watch.

The bird never came back during the day. Where did it live? Where did it come from—the shadows of the forest, the impenetrable depths? No one seemed to know its habits or what timetable it kept to go to those other places, over the isolated spots where it ate and drank. But the boy thought that was as it should be—that no one ought to know. It came from a place that was different, only that. The day: the bird.

Meanwhile his uncle, after receiving a telegram, could not help showing an apprehensive face—hope grown old. But whatever it was, the boy, not wanting to speak of it even to himself, made stubborn by love, must needs repeat over and over silently to himself that his mother was well again, that Mother was safe!

Suddenly he overheard their plan to console him. They

intended to catch the toucan: with a trap, a stone thrown at its beak, a shot in the wing. No, no!—he was angry and distraught. What he loved and wanted could never be that toucan made a prisoner. It was the thin first light of morning, and, within it, that perfect flight.

The hiatus, which in his heart he could now understand, lasted until the next day, when, as it had been each other time, the bird in its radiance was a toy, freely given. Just like the sun; from that little dark point on the horizon, soon fractured with dazzling fire and turned into an eggshell—at the end of the flattened, obscure immensity of the plain, over which one's eyes advanced like an extended arm.

His uncle stood in front of him without saying a word. The boy refused to understand that there was any danger. Within what he was, he said and repeated: his mother had never been sick, she had always been borne safe and sound! The bird's flight filled his whole being. The monkey doll had almost fallen and been lost: its little pointed face and half of its body were hanging out of the pocket when it was caught! The boy had not given it a scolding. The return of the bird was a passion that had been sent to him, an impression of the senses, an overflowing of the heart, until the afternoon. The boy thought of nothing but the toucan in happy flight, in the resounding air. It would console him and ease his sadness so that he could escape the weight of those checkered days.

On the fourth day a telegram came. Uncle smiled, *fortissimo*. His mother was well, she was cured! Next day—after the last toucan sun—they would go back home.

The Moment out of Time

Some time later, the boy was peering out of the window of the plane at the white fraying clouds, the swift emptiness. At the same time, he felt as if he were being left behind to feel homesick, loyal to what was back there in the clearing. To the toucan and the dawn—but to everything else, too, which was a part of those worst days: the house, its people, the forest, the jeep, the dust, the breathless nights—all of that was purified, now, into the almost-blue of his imagining. Life itself never stopped. His uncle, wearing another tie, not as pretty a one, looked at his watch, impatient to arrive. The boy was thinking with half his mind, already almost at the borders of sleep. A sudden gravity made his little face seem longer.

He almost jumped out of his seat with anguish: the little monkey doll wasn't in his pocket! He had gone and lost his little monkey comrade! How could he have done it? Ready tears sprang to his eyes.

But then the pilot's helper came and brought something to comfort him: "Looky here, see what I found for you"—and it was the little red hat with the tall feather, no longer wrinkled, that he had so thoroughly thrown away on the first flight!

The boy could no longer torment himself by crying. But being in the plane with all the noise made him dizzy. He picked up the lonely little hat, smoothed it with his fingers, and put it in his pocket. No, his little monkey companion was not lost in the bottomless darkness of the world, nor ever would be. Surely it was just off having a good time, peradventure, perchance, in the other-place, where people and things were forever coming and going. The boy smiled at what had made him smile, as he suddenly felt like doing: out beyond primordial chaos, like a discreated nebula.

And then came the never-to-be-forgotten stroke of ecstasy by which he was transported, at perfect peace, at oneness. It lasted the barest second, not even that, and crumbled to dust like straw, for evanescence is its very nature and no man can contain it: the whole picture escapes the boundaries of its frame. It was as though he were with Mother, healthy, safe, and smiling, along with the others, and the little monkey with a pretty green necktie—on the porch of the yard full of tall trees . . . and the good old jouncy jeep . . . and every place . . . all at the same time . . . the first stroke of day . . . where time after time they watched the sun's rebirth and—still more vivid, full of sound and living—in unending suspension—the flight of the toucan, as he came to eat berries in the golden treetop, in the high valleys of the dawn, there close to the house. Only that. Only everything.

"Well, we're here at last!" Uncle said.

"Oh, no. Not yet . . ." replied the boy.

He smiled a secret smile: smiles and enigmas, all his own. And life was coming toward him.

A NOTE ABOUT THE AUTHOR

João Guimarães Rosa was born in Cordisburgo, Minas Gerais, Brazil, in 1908, and died in Rio de Janeiro in 1967. He studied medicine and practiced both as a country doctor in the backlands and as a military doctor, taking part in the civil war of 1932. In 1934 he embarked upon a diplomatic career. From 1938 to 1942 he was Brazilian Consul in Hamburg, Germany; from 1942 to 1944, Secretary of the Brazilian Embassy in Bogotá, Colombia; from 1948 to 1951, Embassy Counselor at Paris. He then headed a service of the Ministry of Foreign Affairs. Notable among his works are *Sagarana,* 1946 (English translation, 1966); *Corpo de Baile,* 1956; *Grande Sertão: Veredas,* 1956 (*The Devil to Pay in the Backlands,* 1963); and *Primeiras Estórias,* 1962 (*The Third Bank of the River and Other Stories,* 1968). Shortly before his death, Guimarães Rosa became a member of the Brazilian Academy of Letters.

A NOTE ON THE TYPE

The text of this book was set on the Linotype in a new face called Primer, designed by Rudolph Ruzicka, earlier responsible for the design of Fairfield and Fairfield Medium, Linotype faces whose virtues have for some time now been accorded wide recognition.

The complete range of sizes of Primer was first made available in 1954, although the pilot size of 12 point was ready as early as 1951. The design of the face makes general reference to Linotype Century (long a serviceable type, totally lacking in manner or frills of any kind) but brilliantly corrects the characterless quality of that face.

This book was composed, printed, and bound by American Book–Stratford Press, Inc., New York. Typography by Joan Bastone.